BEAUTIFUL, ONCE

MIA DALIA

PUBLISHED BY CRYSTAL LAKE PUBLISHING
WHERE STORIES COME ALIVE!

Crystal Lake Publishing
www.CrystalLakePub.com

Follow us on Amazon:

WELCOME
TO ANOTHER

CRYSTAL LAKE PUBLISHING
CREATION

Join today at www.crystallakepub.com & www.patreon.com/CLP

For Chelsea. Beautiful, always.

PROLOGUE.

IN ALL HER YEARS specializing in grief psychology and working with survivors, Olivia Thomas had never encountered a case like this. She had never witnessed such darkness in the eyes of another.

Of course, every case was different, just as the traditional five stages of grief were, in her experience, a set of directions rather than a road map. But there was usually more *something*. More give, perhaps.

The person before her looked like how she had always imagined zombies might. Not the zombies of the TV shows and comic books her son was obsessed with, but the real deal. Someone who was dead and alive at the same time.

Olivia had read about this survivor's ordeal, but facts on paper could not and did not adequately prepare her for the sheer wreckage of a person she beheld.

It was as if the experience had rendered the person ageless, genderless. Nearly lifeless. Barely a person at all—more like raw anguish wearing human skin.

If not for the heartbeat, if not for the occasional blinking, they could have been a mannequin sitting across the table.

A wildly unprofessional thought crossed her mind: If someone had ventured so far over to the other side, did she have the strength to pull them back? Did she have the right?

She chastised herself. Of course she had the right. It was her job, her duty, as a healer, as a fellow human being.

"Hello," she said softly with just a hint of a friendly smile. "My name is Olivia. I was hoping we could talk today for a bit."

Her words went as unregistered as her presence. The person before her was caught up in their own world. A dark world, Olivia imagined, at odds with the sunny afternoon outside the windows.

"I've read what happened to you," she continued. "I'm terribly sorry. In my experience, sometimes it helps to talk about it."

Nothing. Silence. According to Olivia's records, the person hadn't said a word.

They hardly ate or drank. Nothing about their demeanor or actions made it seem like they were glad to be alive. The survivor was stronger now than when first found—wasting away, delirious, severely sunburned, dehydrated, and malnourished. Their skin had healed since then, the worst of it anyway, settling into an unhappy shade of reddish brown that reminded Olivia of dried blood. But the mind, invisible, often unreachable, was another matter altogether. And it scarred like no other part of a person.

When it came to survivors, Olivia had witnessed shock, incredulity, anger, guilt, gratitude. There was no singular universal response. It was all simply too much for one's system to handle— the impossibly cruel twist of fate that put them at the heart of a tragedy, and the seemingly random, dramatically kind stroke of luck that had saved them. How could one process such a thing?

The person before her didn't seem interested in processing any of it.

"I can't pretend to know what you've been through, or what

you're currently going through, but I have spoken to a lot of survivors over the years. I could, perhaps, offer some perspective."

The person across the table moved their head. Though a slight, barely perceptible motion, a blink-and-you-miss-it movement, it was something. Encouraged, Olivia pushed on, but she could see her words failing, falling to the ground like weakly shot arrows.

She had to go with the ace up her sleeve: violating the institution's policy.

"I've brought someone here to see you."

No reaction. But did Olivia see a flicker of interest?

Olivia pressed a button on her phone. Shortly after, the door opened, and an orderly walked in with a dog—a large, shaggy mutt with a graying snout. He seemed remarkably friendly considering what he'd been through. Children and animals, you had to admire their resilience. Seemed like anything and anyone that stood taller than a foot or two off the ground couldn't be broken too easily.

The dog had no tag, no name. He was found along with the person, both survivors of the same ordeal. The dog was in much better shape, and after a brief recuperation, seemed strong and lively. He was staying with one of the people who found him, likely to be permanently adopted if the person he'd been found with continued to show no signs of recovery.

The dog, nicknamed Spark by one of the rescuers—aspirationally at first but now living up to it—came in tentatively, his eyes on the person in the chair. He didn't approach and instead stayed by the door. Slowly, softly he began to growl, pawing at the floor.

"Spark, come on," said the orderly under his breath. "Behave."

Olivia watched the face of the person across from her. Watched their head turn toward the dog—an eerily robotic motion.

The dog barked sharply. It served as a slap, a bucket of ice water in the face. Suddenly, the survivor's eyes sprung wide open, animating with something Olivia couldn't quite read. It sent a stirring of alarm dragging a nail down her spine.

When those eyes locked on hers, Olivia thought she could see the flames flickering there. But surely, that was merely a trick of the light, only the sun pouring through the uncurtained window.

"There you are," Olivia said gently. "How are you? How do you feel?"

The person opened their mouth, licked their lips, and closed it again, as if they had forgotten how to speak.

Finally, in a voice rusted out from disuse they croaked a single word: "Hungry." Then, suddenly, with alarming speed and agility, the survivor lunged across the table at Olivia.

The dog began barking in earnest.

"Hungry," the terrible voice repeated so closely to Olivia's ear so that she felt the fiery heat of it. And then the feeding began.

CHAPTER 1.
JACOB.

JACOB GURLEY WAS awakened by the loudest noise he had ever heard. The island was a quiet place, its predawn calm seldom shattered by anything more raucous than a bird song. And much like the darkness made the light appear all the brighter, the silence made the noise seem deafening. It was the sort of thing Jacob had always imagined when reading the words "sonic boom."

It startled him, sending his heart racing against its bony prison in a frantic, panicked manner. He'd always gotten up slowly, relishing the few minutes of perfect peace before the day descended with all its tasks and obligations. He'd lie in bed, studying the patterns of light on the ceiling, as his dreams faded into the ether, allowing reality to set in.

Now Jacob was up, though. Awoken fully and rudely. He padded across the creaky floorboards to the window and peered outside. The sky was light blue, almost white, with a thick stripe of an early morning two-tone orange across. And there was something else there, too. He rubbed his eyes, willing them to focus. His vision hadn't been the same since he turned forty. But there it was, unmissable, a fiery red contrail, its arc pointing downward, toward the farthest end of the island.

A plane—that was Jacob's first thought. But no, he shook his head, peeling away the cobwebs of sleep. It couldn't have been. The sky above the island was a no-fly zone. Some of the younger people here had never even seen a real plane before.

Jacob had. He'd flown to Paris after college and bummed around Europe for months before running out of money and getting tired of not fitting in. The feeling had only intensified over the years, no matter where he was or how ordinary he tried to be. Forever a square peg. Or some shape infinitely more difficult to describe. Finding the island had changed his life. It was the first place he'd ever truly belonged. It was his home; he *felt* at home here.

That sense of protectiveness drove his socked feet into his boots and his booted feet into the street before fear or caution even had a chance of setting in. Jacob had to know what the noise was.

He wasn't the only one who'd been woken up, or had gotten the idea to investigate. The portly form of Terrence Cauley—clad in a ratty, once-blue robe—bobbed up and down on his front porch, peering at the distance.

"Terry."

"Jacob. What the heck was that?"

"Beats me."

The morning was brisk. The summer tiptoed its way onto the island reluctantly this year. It didn't warm up until well into the afternoon, and the early mornings still firmly belonged to the remnants of a moody spring. Jacob's thin old T-shirt and jersey pajama bottoms did nothing to keep him warm. He shivered and rubbed his arms.

"Do you have binoculars?" Terry asked. Their porches were only a few feet apart, but the big man projected his speech. Years of working construction back on the mainland had damaged his hearing.

"No," Jacob replied.

"Me neither." Terry sighed and rubbed his forehead with the back of a meaty paw. "Wish I did now. Is that smoke?"

Jacob squinted. He could just barely make out a thin column of smoke rising up from behind the trees; it billowed far away, probably from the place the red contrail had descended.

Martha Geller came out of her house. Despite the hour, the woman was so put together Jacob couldn't help but wonder what time she got out of bed every morning—not a hair out of place, outfit neat. She'd probably had her morning coffee already.

"Gentlemen."

They nodded at her, almost in unison. She'd been a high school principal on the mainland, and the demeanor and bearing stuck. Martha was a woman who, in the words of Jacob's ex, did not suffer fools gladly.

With the school on the island being a much smaller and more organic learning environment, Martha turned her indomitable disciplinarian spirit to other matters. She was Ronan's second-in-command, his far-reaching and ever-powerful right hand.

"What was that?" she inquired matter-of-factly.

Hers was the third house by the shared public garden on their tiny makeshift cul-de-sac. Small and closely spaced out like most buildings on the island, the setup allowed for just the right balance of privacy and community. Here, you *had* to like your neighbors; but most of them were easy to like. Credit where credit was due— Ronan's prescreenings really did work.

"No idea," Terry said, pulling the lapels of his robe closer together.

Martha turned her steely gray eyes to Jacob.

He shrugged. "I think someone should go look."

She stared at him some more, until he amended his phrasing. "I think we should go look."

"Great idea." She rewarded him with a smile she must have once reserved for bright but unruly schoolchildren. "I'll speak with Ronan and let him know."

Jacob sighed and dragged himself back into the house to change. This was obviously going to be one of those mornings.

He'd never been good at going with the flow. Back on the mainland, anything perceived as a wrench thrown into the carefully wound and maintained cogs of his life gave him panic attacks. He managed them—and the crippling anxiety—with a combination of benzodiazepines and drinking. The two shouldn't have gone together, but it worked. Well enough, anyway. On the rare occasions when benzos failed and booze betrayed, Jacob resorted to bad decisions: one-night stands and the like.

Being on the island, he'd slowly weaned off his dependencies, yet the ghostly echoes of them remained, occasionally triggered still. The sonic boom, for instance, had triggered him. Going to look for its source was proactive but fraught with uncertainty. Anything with uncertain results was grounds for panic.

It was one of the reasons he had come to the island in the first place. There was a beguiling simplicity to life here. A precision-cut scarcity of options that left choices clear and easy.

Jacob relished it. The cost it came with was well worth it to him. Except for mornings like these.

He rolled a crystal deodorant stick under his arms in lieu of a shower and pulled on a pair of jeans and a sweatshirt with a faded university logo. He chugged a glass of water, swirling it around his mouth to get rid of his cottonmouth, and tied the shoelaces of his boots. Almost presentable. After a second thought, Jacob put on his windbreaker. It was probably overkill, but the old thing was waterproof, had tons of pockets, and would keep him warm until the sun properly woke up to do its job. Finally, he put on his watch, grabbed his keys, and stepped outside.

Terry was already there. For a big man, he moved surprisingly fast. Jacob had always imagined his neighbor as a former football star, with mountains of muscles hiding under a thick slab of fat. He was tall, too, standing nearly half a foot over Jacob's not too shabby five-eleven.

"Ready?" Terry asked. He had changed into a pair of bright red tracksuit bottoms and a lightweight yellow fleece. His hiking boots were a modest dark gray.

He also wore a trucker hat advertising a pizza joint Jacob had never heard of. Then again, in all the years Jacob had known him, Terry had always been an eclectic dresser. He'd even found time to shave somehow while Jacob's face remained stubbly. He'd been pretty diligent about shaving ever since the gray began creeping into his facial hair, making him look and feel old, but this morning he just didn't have the time, desire, or coordination to pick up a razor.

Martha was already gone. The woman was married to her job. By all accounts, a happy marriage, too.

"Ready," Jacob said, not feeling it. The undercurrents of anxiety stirred in his gut and scratched their jagged nails across his amygdala.

The two men walked. The island was slowly waking up all

around them. The normally peaceful and bucolic scene had also been stirred by the rude awakening. People went about their business, but there was only one topic to their conversations, only one thing on their minds.

"The natives are restless," Terry joked. "We should walk faster."

"I think you mean, *I* should walk faster," Jacob joked back. "Sorry, man. I'm just . . ."

"Not a morning person?"

"I was going to say not a quest person." Jacob made sure to raise his voice just enough when he spoke for his neighbor to hear him comfortably.

Terry laughed—a booming sound. Put that into an amplifier, crank the machine up, and you'd get the mystery noise that woke them up earlier.

"Did you see the thing?" Jacob asked. "In the sky. Right when it happened."

"You mean the red swoosh thingy?"

"Yeah, like a contrail."

"Yep. That's what makes me think I know what this thing is out there," Terry said with confidence.

Jacob waited a beat. "Are you going to tell me or make me guess in twenty questions?"

"Ha. Sure, I'll tell you." Terry adjusted the bill of his hat. "I think it's some sort of space debris. People are too busy tossing their toys and crap all over creation, down here and up there," he jacked a meaty thumb skyward, "And what goes up . . ." Using his heavily muscled arms, Terry made a motion of an object dropping, powerful enough to displace air in its wake.

"You mean, like a satellite?"

"Anything, really. Space exploration is a messy business." Terry shook his massive head. "You know they leave bags of poop on the Moon? How's that for making a good first impression?"

Jacob laughed.

Terry went on. "Things in space are constantly burning up, crashing, breaking apart, and it's all falling down here. Ronan can only protect the airspace above us so much."

Jacob still wasn't sure how that worked. Before coming to the island, he had never heard of such a thing as restricted air space for private use. It must have cost a fortune, but Ronan's finances were as mysterious as the man himself. And just as open to speculation.

"You know, before I stopped bothering with the news, I read they were thinking of building hotels in space. Imagine that?"

Jacob shook his head. He couldn't. He'd never been particularly imaginative. All his entertainment choices were solidly reality based. He'd never met a science fiction or a fantasy story he enjoyed, in any format.

"We're talking like these giant rotating habitable cylinders that make their own gravity," Terry continued, talking with his hands.

"I bet the views would be nice," Jacob mused.

"Sure, yeah, the views. But doesn't make it right. You wanna mine asteroids and whatnot for things we need here on Earth, that's one thing, but no one needs a hotel in space. It's just . . ." Terry searched for a word and spat out "wasteful" in the end.

Jacob thought about it. In principle, he agreed. Wastefulness was abhorred on the island. The concept Terry had described was objectively fun to contemplate and in no small way distracted Jacob from his gnawing, low-grade anxiety, but in reality, it was nothing but another thing for the one percent crowd to amuse themselves. Did people still say that back on the mainland? The one percent? Or was there a new catchall name for the ultra wealthy?

Following the news wasn't prohibited on the island by any means, merely discouraged. You couldn't go forward if you spent so much time looking back, as Ronan would say. Why drag the ugliness of all you left behind here, into this new Eden?

Jacob didn't miss it, not really. *The New York Times* digest he used to read every morning while he ate his toast and eggs—rye and over easy respectively—never failed to depress him. The news was hopeless; the trends were unfathomable; the celebrities were famous for less and less.

It was better to leave it all behind. He'd been glad to. They all were. And now a piece of that world had found them all the way out here, crashing in like an uninvited guest.

"What would they do with all the poop?" he asked Terry. "The space hotel people."

The big man thought about it, pushing back his trucker hat to scratch his shaved head. "You know something? I have no idea," he said, laughing.

The island still had room for expansion, both agriculturally and in population. Ronan had been careful not to overdo things. It was all about balance and finding what was fit: the right people, the right crops, the right opportunities.

There was something refreshing in how much of the island still belonged to Mother Nature, unclaimed and untamed. Soon, Jacob and Terry left civilization behind as they proceeded through the woody terrain.

Here, with the trees' canopies shading them from the sun, Jacob was glad for his windbreaker. Terry, like most men his size, seemed impervious to weather, but the bite in the air made Jacob shiver.

Their steps were absorbed by the mossy ground beneath them, all dead leaves and rain-moistened soil. It sucked at their shoes, but not enough to pull them under or even slow them down.

Terry got out a small packet of food and offered some to Jacob. "What is it?"

"Mushroom jerky. Sandy made it."

While tempting, it was categorically the wrong flavor and texture for breakfast. "No, thanks."

Terry shrugged. "More for me," he said cheerfully, sticking one of the shriveled-up sticks into his mouth like a weird skinny cigar. In all the time Jacob had known his neighbor, the big man had never gone without eating for longer than half an hour. If it was a coping mechanism, it worked like a charm. Terry seldom seemed in low spirits.

Jacob's stomach did not appear to get the memo about what constituted appropriate breakfast foods and growled its displeasure. He elbowed it.

Out here, in nature—with his jolly neighbor by his side and sunlight streaking tentatively through the trees—it was easy to dismiss the fear Jacob felt all morning after hearing the loud noise.

That was the very meaning of the community—a weight shared was a weight halved. Ronan always talked about it, and he was right. Jacob had felt lighter since coming to the island. It was a magnificently powerful feeling, this sense of belonging. He'd been reluctant to trust it at first, but slowly he gave in, accepting it gratefully like a gift you always wanted but never let yourself have. Being on the island didn't shave off the corners of Jacob's square pegs—it made the entire rubric irrelevant.

Jacob had first heard about the island online and dismissed it as a rumor, or a bit of weird news. He did not give it a second thought until a work colleague brought it up. Her daughter, she said, had found a home there. The young woman who'd been in and out of trouble and rehab centers for most of her adult life had found a place to settle down and be happy.

It made Jacob look into the island more seriously, dig around, do some research. Still, it was months—

"What's that smell?" Terry cut through Jacob's reverie. "You smell it? What is that?"

Now that Terry mentioned it, there *was* a smell. Jacob couldn't place it for the life of him. It seemed organic but not like anything that surrounded them. It was sharper, more pungent, with a minor note that hit your tear ducts as potently as a freshly cut onion.

"I've no idea," Jacob replied, scratching his nose. "It's weird."

"Yeah," Terry echoed. "Very weird. Must be getting closer."

They had originally followed the smoke column, but it faded as they walked, all but disappearing from view by now. Jacob looked up, just to check, not watching where he was going. The tall treetops made him dizzy. He'd never been much for nature. He blamed it on a fear of ticks, but it was more than that. The great outdoors had just never seemed that great. Less so now with a mystery inside them.

"What the—" Terry exclaimed.

Jacob's head snapped back from the clouds to the strange sight before them. The forest out here was flattened as if giants had walked through it, trampling the trees around them as easily as children might do with grass. However, this flattened earth appeared to have a discernible pattern of concentric circles. The eye at its center, about the size of a soccer ball or a little smaller, sat half-embedded in the ground and glowed an unearthly hue. It seemed impossible that its fall could have caused such devastating damage, yet the evidence proved the contrary.

Nature itself had bowed down to the force of this mysterious sphere, creating a clearing as structured as a worship site. The air immediately surrounding the sphere crawled with thin tendrils of acrid smoke. The object, though relatively small, had a malevolent presence about it. This sort of thing made Jacob's anxiety roar like a simmering fire that had been fed fresh logs. The feeling ripped up his guts, whispering worst-case scenarios into his ears.

The smell was stronger here. Hands went up to cover faces, eyes teared.

"Well, hell," Terry said finally. "I'm pretty sure that's no space turd."

CHAPTER 2.
MARTHA.

MARTHA GELLER COULD not remember a time when she did not like rules. They'd been her comfort, her guiding light, her raison d'être, even when they caused her the ridicule and scorn of her peers. Even when they prevented her from being socially accepted.

Frankly, she didn't know how Ronan would ever manage to run the place without her firm hand beside his, holding the reins. He was a dreamer, a big idea man, a romantic. Martha recognized it immediately upon meeting him. Her father had been the same. She watched year after year as life eroded her dad's beautiful spirit and vowed to never let it happen to her. Her mother was a plain woman with a face etched by the fine lines of disappointment and lips permanently pursed in tacit disapproval. She never got over the fact that the lovely boy she married failed to mature into a steady rock of a man she could happily chain herself to. Nor did she understand her serious, studious daughter who never cared to play with dolls.

It resulted in the Gellers being three separate entities, unfathomable to one another, and thus never congealing into a cohesive unit like other families.

BEAUTIFUL, ONCE

Martha left home at seventeen, after skipping a grade and graduating early. She went from one college to another, earning the degrees necessary to secure herself a position where she could have a strictly delineated, rule-based position.

Being a high school principal suited her at first, back when she still thought she could make a difference. After her youthful naivete dissipated, Martha realized that her chaotic workplace and her unruly charges resented discipline just as much as they needed it. And they needed it a lot.

They didn't like her and didn't bother making a secret of it. The staff thought she was dry and humorless. The kids thought worse. They'd taken to calling her Adolf, the cruelty of it accentuated by the fact that she was Jewish.

She persevered out of sheer stubbornness, and because having dedicated so much time to her career, she hardly had anything else in her life. She had a cactus once that was good company and provided exactly the right amount of affection. Then the cactus died, and Martha didn't have the heart to get another one. She began looking for alternative sources of solace and eventually found Ronan. Or rather they found each other.

He was good looking. That was the first thing Martha noticed about him. It was impossible to ignore. Ronan was one of those rare creatures blessed both with beauty and the good graces to wear it well. He had an easy smile, a twinkle in his blue eyes, and movie-star-quality dirty blond hair.

Martha had never had much interest in men. Or women, for that matter. Relationships seemed messy. Besides, she'd never found anyone who met her standards; if she did, she was pretty sure they wouldn't be interested in a short, frizzy-haired woman with cankles and a bitter heart.

It wasn't an attraction with Ronan, per se. She didn't want to take him to bed. She simply wanted to be around him.

They met at a book reading. The latest hotshot political pundit was pushing his views around, cladding them in buzzwords. When Ronan noticed her looking his way, he rolled his eyes and made a funny gesture with his hand, making it into a fist and extending the pointer and pinkie fingers. She didn't know what it meant. Something to do with rock 'n' roll? But she liked the moment of attention; it felt as bright and warm as sunlight.

Afterward, she saw him outside the library.

"You didn't buy the book?" he said, grinning.

"Oh, no, I wouldn't." She frantically thought of something clever to say. "It's an offense to trees."

He laughed, rather more than the joke merited, but Martha liked that. Emboldened, she asked, "What does that mean?" She repeated his hand gesture from earlier.

"Oh. That's American Sign Language for bullshit."

She must have blushed, for he smiled kindly. "I forgot the word for balloon," he explained. "But that guy was full of hot air."

"He was," Martha agreed. "It's a shame he has such a platform."

"We live in a world where all the wrong people get all the best platforms," he said wistfully. "Shame, don't you think? What this world is turning into?"

"Shame," she agreed. She wanted to agree with this man, just to keep him standing there, talking. She liked the way he looked at her, without judgment, without reservation.

"I'm Ronan," he said, offering her his hand.

She shook, finding it was warm and strong without being forceful. She felt the calluses on his palm.

"Martha Geller," she introduced herself automatically.

"Well, Martha Geller," Ronan said smiling again. "What would you say, given a platform?"

She could do prepared speeches and PowerPoint presentations; she could enforce the school's rules on the spot, but spontaneous openness and ad-libbing had never been her strength.

She utilized the only conversational trick she knew and turned it around. "What would *you* say?"

They went for coffee, and he told her. Ronan, as it turned out, had a lot of things to say.

Martha had been listening to them ever since. And finding ways to implement them.

Over the years, their relationship had evolved into a close partnership that managed to avoid any romantic undertones. It was easier that way, cleaner.

And because it was easy, Martha found herself opening up, even joking around, letting Ronan see the side of her she had kept hidden for so long she wasn't sure it still existed.

Being yourself, it seemed, was like riding a bicycle. You never forgot.

When Ronan's idealism ballooned him, she held the string and anchored him. When Martha's strict nature threatened to turn her pedantic and unlikable, Ronan stepped in, brightened her demeanor, and smoothed away her edges.

They were the proverbial odd couple, but it worked. Just look at what they had been able to accomplish together.

Sure, this place had been Ronan's dream—and seeded with his money—but it would have never gotten on track or functioned as beautifully as it did without Martha's steady guiding hand. She quite literally wrote the original handbook for the new arrivals. Not a rule book or a guidebook, Ronan corrected, not a manual, merely something you could put into another person's hand and say, "Here. This is how our world works."

Ronan did the recruiting originally, sure. She'd never had the charm, perseverance, or stamina for that. But once people arrived, they needed help setting up, and that was where Martha excelled.

When they first met for coffee, Ronan told her of a vision for a different way of life; for time spent meaningfully, surrounded by like-minded individuals. A place where people who felt betrayed by their society and their politicians could come and feel seen and heard.

"You're talking about a cult, then?" she asked, narrowing her eyes, still unsure what to make of this irresistible stranger.

He laughed. "No, nothing like that. A commune at most."

"Is there a difference?" she bantered back.

"Of course, there is," he protested over his mug of hot chocolate.

And it was easy to believe him because she already liked him by then, everything from his laugh to his choice of beverage.

"So you have no intention of sleeping with every female there?" she asked, surprising herself with her boldness, regretting her choice of words. Who said *female*? It was so . . . biology textbook.

"I won't sleep with any," Ronan said, holding up a three-fingered salute. "I don't really do that."

Gay, Martha thought. Well, that figured. All the best looking men always were.

"I'm in mourning," he explained as if reading her mind. "So I guess I'm celibate for the time being."

"Oh," Martha said, lowering her eyes.

"There I go oversharing again." He chuckled. "Sorry about that. Just wanted you to know what sort of a person I was."

"But I already know," she wanted to say. "You're good. A good person." She believed in first impressions implicitly, but this certainty was still unusual. It was almost like fate.

They talked more, until their drinks were nothing but distant memories and they had to order more to keep their table. By the time they left, Martha felt sure that at long last she had made a real friend.

Here on the island, Martha woke up every day at 5:30 a.m. She did stretches, showered, ate her breakfast of porridge with granola and fresh fruit topping, drank her coffee, and planned the day ahead. There were always tasks, exactly how she liked it. Idle hands and all that.

Ronan was a restless sleeper, frequently staying up half the night and sleeping in late. She often made it to his place before he was up and set about starting his coffeemaker and sorting his mail. He trusted her completely; she'd had the key to his house for years.

He had it built shortly after acquiring the island and then modified it through the years. Without anything like a unifying design, the place looked a bit mad from the outside, though once inside, you saw that everything made sense. Well, it did to the man who lived there, anyway.

The top floor was convertible. Ronan loved sleeping under the stars, weather permitting. Downstairs was taken up by a kitchen, bathroom, and sitting room. The office space was added in the back of the property, almost as an afterthought, when the dining table could no longer hold their paperwork.

It was surprising how much paperwork the place required. All these statements of visibility for people who only wanted to be invisible.

Legally speaking, the island was a nation unto itself, serving as proof of how far money could go when the right palms were greased.

It was sovereign enough to be left alone, unimportant enough to be forgotten, and too small to make it onto most maps. Just as they wanted.

The airspace buy was a big one. Ronan insisted there was no way to leave the world behind and have routine and noisy flights overhead. He felt the same way about the internet and most modern technology, but he wasn't a Luddite. Ronan understood and appreciated what it offered; he simply sought to decrease dependency on it.

The internet, for instance, was readily available for research, but not social media. Video games were frowned upon unless they had educational value or fitness benefits.

Having seen firsthand the detrimental effects of both social media and video games on her young charges back in her principal days, Martha was glad for the restrictions. Sure enough, the children on the island were better off than the ones she used to work with: smarter, more focused and polite, less stressed.

Here, kids played games outside, ones Martha could recognize and understand. They seemed younger, or perhaps merely free to act their age, and categorically happier. It was a big draw for parents, for families.

However, the majority of the island consisted of a strong singles population. People who failed to fit in back on the mainland found their home here. Just like she did.

Ronan had envisioned it precisely like this. "The island of misfit toys," he'd joke, half-kidding.

It was difficult for Martha to imagine back then how someone like Ronan could ever have a problem fitting in anywhere, but later, as she got to know him, she saw how much his charisma served as a heavy suit of armor, and he eagerly discarded it at the end of the day.

Ronan was an extroverted introvert, someone who turned on the magic on demand, and shut it down gratefully when it was no longer needed, retreating into a corner to recharge in solitude.

He trusted her to take over the reins while he was resting. Martha relished the responsibility.

There was so much to do at first. All the permits, the legal hurdles, the endless logistics, the ceaseless construction work. Most of it related to things she had dealt with in her previous line of work. She had long since lost faith in the modern education system, at least in public schools. Here was something new, something to believe in.

Ronan asked her to put in her resignation at school a month after they met. She was trembling when she typed the letter up, unsure if her nerves were because of fear or excitement.

Ronan then hired her full time, and they began their work in earnest.

Hard to imagine how many years had passed. Time had simply flown by. She'd sometimes see the first-generation kids all grown up, or the trees they planted upon arrival now tall and fruit bearing. She'd think, "Wow, look how long it's been."

She didn't much feel the weight of the years. Her diet had been better on the island than on the mainland. She was able to maintain the same weight, more or less. Her hair started to gray, but Carrie, the preeminent hairdresser on the island, had taken to using henna on it so one couldn't really tell. As middle age advanced and swept her away, Martha, who had never looked particularly young, realized she didn't look particularly old either.

She simply had one of those faces—perpetually a woman of a certain age.

Ronan, on the other hand, didn't seem to age at all. She always joked about the portrait he probably kept in his attic. Sure, if you looked closely, there were more wrinkles now, but his eyes still twinkled, his smile still dazzled. And somehow, his hair remained blond. Carrie swore she had nothing to do with it. Magic, indeed.

Martha had never been sure of Ronan's age before, and she grew even less sure with time. He was younger than her, sure, but an old soul. She'd been prone to mothering him from time to time but didn't think their age difference was that extensive. He was more like the younger brother she never had. That's how she liked to think of it. Their dynamic was a cross between siblings and a leader and his second-in-command. No real boundaries, though. They never needed any.

Ronan gave her a job she could be happily married to and a place to call home. In return, Martha gave him everything she had to give. It seemed fair.

The noise that morning hadn't woken her up. She was already showered and halfway through breakfast. It did startle her, though. The sudden loudness of it shook her and made her drop her spoon, which made a piercing, clattering sound and splattered her blouse with the bit of porridge it trebucheted in its fall.

Martha frowned and went to get a wet cloth to dab at the stain before it had a chance to set in. What was that? The island was too quiet of a place for such things. This was an oasis away from the infernal racket of the mainland.

In the end, she decided to change blouses, letting her other shirt soak properly, and stepped outside, her curiosity finally winning over.

BEAUTIFUL, ONCE

It better not be something crazy Ronan's cooked up as a surprise, she thought. He'd done wild things before when he got restless. Martha didn't care for such unscheduled disruptions—especially not this week.

She wasn't the first one out of the door. Jacob and Terry had beat her to it. Nice guys, both of them. She had personally approved their residency applications. There were some perks to her position of power, after all. For one thing, she got to choose her neighbors.

The two men were opposites in a way: Jacob thin and quiet, with dark hair perpetually in need of a trim, and Terry, a great giant of a man with a large, shaved head—a talker with a friendly grin always at the ready. They had all spent time together in social situations. Martha knew more about them than they did about her, and she very much liked that imbalance. Besides, there wasn't a lot to her life, certainly not enough to share.

She felt sometimes that her personal trajectory had been too plain, from her parents' home to academia to work to Ronan. Not enough curves and tributaries like the rivers of other lives.

Martha had read their applications and marveled at the complexities of their lives, the serpentine twists and turns of them. But for them and for her, the island was the Rome all roads led to.

She knew of the doping scandal that ended Terry's professional sports career and of Jacob's troubles, but that knowledge was purely academic. She'd never bring it up unless they did. Everyone got a fresh start on the island; that was the beauty of it. The real world promised reinvention but never made good on it. Everyone was always trudging along, dragging the carcasses of their past behind them. Everyone remained marked by their sins enshrined in the ever-present internet. No one forgiven, nothing forgotten.

The promises of that world were mere illusions. And illusions left you disillusioned, as Ronan liked to say.

The island handed you a tabula rasa as a welcome mat. "Here," it said. "Who do you want to be?"

Martha chose to be a productive, useful, important person. It made her happy.

Terry Cauley and Jacob Gurley chose to be nice guys, a baker and a mechanic.

Much better than the neighbors she had back on the mainland: a taciturn elderly couple, rendered genderless and nearly indistinguishable from one another by time and wear, and a young couple with too many kids and pets.

Single people, Martha believed, did well around other single people. Especially once they got to a certain age and place in life where their solitude was largely a choice they were comfortable with.

This early in the morning, both Jacob and Terry looked like little boys, confused and startled, still wearing their pajamas. Martha wouldn't be caught dead outside in her nightwear, but to each their own.

She treated them like little boys too, recalling her principal days, telling them what to do in a way that made it seem like it was their own idea to investigate. They could go see what the noise was all about. Martha was curious. She wondered if she should feel alarmed. But nothing had ever happened on the island to cause alarm. It was too quiet a place. Their community, built with the main intent of peace, was peaceful, indeed.

She still locked her door out of habit some days, but she never had to. She couldn't think of anything she owned that someone might covet enough to risk banishment. In all the years since the establishment of their community, there had been a handful of people who left for various personal reasons, and only a single person ever banished. And no one really wanted to talk or think about that.

And so, convincing herself the noise was an odd but easily explainable thing currently being investigated by two people, Martha, content in knowing she had done her best in the situation, retrieved her bag and proceeded to Ronan's.

CHAPTER 3.
ARDEN.

SHE'D NEVER BEEN good at sleeping in new places. Her usual pattern was staying up half the night, tossing and turning on a perfectly comfortable bed that could have been made of rocks for all the difference it made, and then falling into a deep, troubled sleep in the early hours of the morning. The boom startled her awake, and she sat up in bed, heart pounding.

What was that? she thought. What was anything in this place? Less than twenty-four hours on the island, and Arden didn't know what to make of it. It was all so terribly . . . ordinary.

She had, of course, been hoping for just the opposite. Something more along the lines of the terrifying cults from all the multi-episode documentary adaptations dominating TV streaming channels. Arden was looking for the sensational, salacious, spectacular. She quit her alliterative game while she was ahead.

Coming here was her big chance at a real story. Her once-promising career had stalled some time ago, and everyone seemed to be aware of it. It was like a bad smell that followed her around, the sourness of disappointment. Arden panicked and cast her net far and wide to see what she could catch. But she had never hoped to snag a fish like Ronan Bard. No, not a fish—a shark, or a great white whale.

Ronan's island community had only ever made the news for being so not newsworthy. It talked and walked like a cult, but there were never any scandals, lawsuits, or accusations. It was like one of those rare countries that treaded the middle ground so expertly and managed to stay out of the news so consistently you almost forgot it existed.

And yet, Ronan himself was an extraordinary figure, commanding an article or, better yet, an exposé, all of his own. He fascinated Arden. She wielded her name as an icebreaker, her charm as an offering. Still, she was surprised when he said yes. Shocked. Excited.

She moved all her plans around to schedule her visit as soon as possible before he could change his mind. Now she was here, and it felt so damn underwhelming.

Arden was given her rather unusual name by her Shakespearean-loving, scholarly parents. She told the story as an anecdote and used it on Ronan to highlight their Bard connection. But deep down, she stopped finding it amusing a long time ago, ever since she realized that she must be a disappointment to her family.

They had tried their best to raise a writer; an admirer, a creator, or perhaps a teacher of fiction, but Arden never really cared about make believe. She liked facts, real-life stories—the stranger the better.

She became a journalist, which was the closest she could come to meeting their expectations and staying true to her own interests. But her focus was forever shifting from serious social issues to other, less savory realms. Deep in her heart, Arden loved a good scandal. It got her blood pumping like nothing else. And she would have bet her bottom dollar Ronan Bard was hiding at least one of those until she came to the island and met him.

Maybe he was a good actor. Hell, he could have been with those looks. Nothing about him sounded her alarms. He seemed nice. You couldn't sell stories with that. No one was going to watch six full-length episodes about people living peacefully and mindfully away from it all. No one in this day and age cared about niceness.

What if the booming noise that woke her up was part of a secret? Her mind spun, concocting scenarios with underground labs and secret experiments. You could do just about anything out here and get away with it. The laws on the island were wonky—a firm reminder that in a country run like a business, enough money can buy you just about everything, including near-complete autonomy.

Chris, her boyfriend, had warned her about this, cautioning her on the dangers of a lawless community in a half-mocking tone. They spoke of it often after she decided to go. The last time was the night before she left.

"They have laws," she countered. "They have their own laws. They are not savages."

Chris growled and screwed up his features into a beastly expression. He already had something of a Neanderthal about him with his low, heavy brow and hirsuteness. She thought him funny looking when they first met. His handsomeness only dawned on her later.

They weren't serious enough to live together yet but getting there. They were certainly at a point when his concern for her safety was more than casual.

"I mean it," he said. "Will you be checking in with me or what? I need to know when to send in the troops after you."

"You're being ridiculous," Arden told him, her fingers tangled in the matted fur of his stomach and trailing lower. They were in her bed; she was leaving in the morning, packed bags by the door. They'd already made love once, and she was idly contemplating a second go.

"I did some research," Chris went on, trying to ignore her traveling fingers. "The place is either paradise on Earth or some sort of a top secret horror show."

"Why do you say that?" she asked, poking his belly button.

He emitted a spot-on Pillsbury Dough Boy squeak, making her laugh.

"Because there just isn't enough chatter about it on the internet, and in this day and age, that is the most suspicious thing of all."

Arden shrugged. "Maybe they are Luddites. Happy, happy Luddites. Maybe they've got nothing to share with the world."

Chris did content control for a social media website. He couldn't help but find this all utterly "wonky," to use his word for it.

He arched his eyebrows at her, and she leaned in to kiss his nose. "Let's fuck, worryguts," she said, utilizing her beloved British slang. "You think too much."

Now, she kept coming back to that conversation, Chris's furrowed brow on her mind. Her phone hadn't worked since she got to the island.

"We don't have a cell phone tower, I'm afraid," Ronan explained apologetically. He let her use his satellite phone to let Chris know she had arrived safely, but that was all. She left a voicemail.

When asked about Wi-Fi, she was told it was a complicated

system, something about heavy safety measures. It seemed suspect, but she figured it was Ronan's way of controlling the narrative. A cheap but effective trick.

Still, it left Arden feeling isolated in a way that had nothing to do with geography: vulnerable.

It was surreal to see an entire community of people unglued from tech. No one was on their phones, everyone seemed properly engaged with their environment instead of their devices. She was granted permission to use her phone's camera, but the photos had to be approved by Ronan or that peculiar woman, Martha.

How did that dynamic duo work? Arden wondered upon meeting them. Ronan with his movie star looks and carefree demeanor and Martha, dowdy and strict, tight-lipped and steely-eyed. Surely, they weren't a couple, were they? Arden had seen stranger. Her best friend from college married a man twenty years older and half a foot shorter. True love, it seemed, only made sense to those caught in its net.

Martha handled all the logistics of her visit, and Arden could tell she wasn't happy about any of it. It must have been Ronan's idea. She couldn't imagine Martha welcoming Arden's prying eyes. The woman seemed more like a dragon, a keeper and protector of the treasures. Serious and briskly efficient, she possessed a demeanor that brought to mind old-fashioned words like schoolmarm or spinster.

Martha was the one who put her up in this small guest house behind Ronan's place.

"Do you get guests often?" Arden asked, trying to keep the sarcasm out of her voice.

Martha frowned slightly. "This is Ronan's office of sorts," she explained, and that was that.

The place had a narrow bed, a desk, and a chair. It had a small bathroom with a stall shower in one corner. Practically spartan.

There was no closet, no clothing rail, no dresser. She'd have to live out of her suitcase.

The craggy man in yellow waterproof overalls who brought her here in a boat didn't have much to say about the place besides, "Nice people."

Arden wondered if Ronan paid him for his discretion.

For meals, Arden had to go to the main house. She wondered what Ronan would be like first thing in the morning: bright-eyed and bushy-tailed, or surly and walleyed? She wondered what he would look like in his pajamas. She shouldn't wonder, she knew, but she couldn't help it. Beauty was like that, an invasive species through and through. It got inside your brain, rearranging your thoughts.

Ronan was as different from Chris as two males of the same species could be, but Arden had never had a type. In high school, it was punk rockers. In college, emo poets and willowy girls in glasses. Her twenties were largely wasted trying to figure out what she wanted. Shortly after she passed the thirty-year mark and surrendered to the fact that she had no idea, she met Chris.

Yet Ronan had that quality where she would have found him attractive at any age. The ease with which he carried himself, like gravity itself was different for him.

She wasn't going to do anything about it, of course. Maybe a light fantasy or two, but that was it. Otherwise, it would be impartial. She needed this article to sing. Sing her way back to the main stage, under the spotlight. Arden was no good at being a nobody—mediocrity wore her down.

The strange boom sound preyed on her mind. She would have

never given it a second thought in the city, dismissing the noise as a car backfiring, or hitting another car, or one of the million other noise polluters that happened daily. But out here, in this idyllic silence . . .

Arden showered, her elbows hitting the sides of the stall, got dressed in dark skinny jeans and a light blue button-up, and did her makeup, taking care to keep it natural—her "island look." She tried her phone out of habit, stared at the blank screen for a moment, frowning, then stepped outside.

The fresh air made her shiver. It felt like a good ten-degree difference between the mainland and here. She didn't think she was that far north. Maybe it was the breeze from the water. Hugging herself, Arden paced the slightly overgrown yard for a few moments to gather her thoughts, then knocked on the house door.

No answer.

She twisted the knob and opened the door. It wasn't even a surprise—to her the island seemed like the place where people didn't bother with the locks.

"Ronan?" she projected, sticking her head in. "It's Arden."

After a moment of consideration, she let herself in. "Ronan?" she repeated, hearing her voice echo lightly.

The place wasn't big enough to shout. She would just wait. Arden sat down on the sofa and looked around. It was her first time alone in the space. The unpresumptuous coziness of it struck her anew.

Chris's condo was all high tech, everything digitally controlled, screens everywhere. Heavy furniture, dark wood and leather. All very manly and nice enough, though Arden wasn't sure she'd want to live like that day in and day out. It was one of the reasons she never pushed for cohabitation. It seemed like there would be too many compromises. An exhaustive amount of compromises, and just when she got her life designed to her liking.

By comparison, Ronan's place had a kind of earthy vibe to it: live edge wood, light and smooth, and old, broken-in couches, charmingly mismatched. No screens, only an old-fashioned record player. It was a place designed for comfort first and foremost.

The curtains were open, allowing in the milky morning light. Arden knelt down to browse Ronan's neatly arranged records in stacked wooden crates.

"Good morning."

Arden jumped and dropped the old Elvis Costello album she was holding.

"Good morning, Martha."

The woman was likely as stealthy as a ninja to have come in like that. She looked perfectly put together, her lips slightly pursed in what Arden perceived as tacit disapproval. It reminded her of a civics teacher she once had, Ms. Clemmons, altered by absolutely everyone to Ms. Lemon for obvious reasons.

"Sleep well?"

"Kind of. Did you hear that noise?" Arden picked up the album, put it back in its crate, and stood up. An old ex of hers was absolutely obsessed with one of the tracks on that record. The song was all about obsessive love. . . . Talk about red flags.

"Yes, it was rather difficult to miss." Martha quirked her lips into an almost smile.

"What was it?"

"No idea. I've sent some people to go look. I'm sure it's nothing."

"Why?"

"Excuse me?"

"Why are you so sure it's nothing?" Arden pushed. "If you have no idea what it is."

The almost smile vanished. "Because it's always nothing. Here on the island, we don't get much excitement, I'm afraid."

Was that sarcasm? Arden couldn't tell.

"Is Ronan around?" she asked.

"He must be still sleeping. You would be amazed what that man can sleep through."

With that, Martha set about starting coffee and breakfast.

"What do you like to eat first thing in the morning?" she asked Arden without turning around.

"Oh, anything, really. Well, no, not everything. That actually backfired a few times when I traveled. But you know, toast, or cereal, or oatmeal, or eggs." She was babbling, she realized, trying to win this taciturn woman over.

"Where have you traveled?" Martha asked, surprising Arden.

"UK, France, Spain, Australia, Japan, South Africa, Argentina."

"Impressive. Was it for work?" Martha turned around, her face expressionless. The stovetop espresso maker began to gurgle to life behind her.

"Some work, some pleasure," Arden replied.

"And now you're here," Martha said measuredly.

"And now I'm here," Arden echoed brightly. "Perhaps the most exotic place of all."

Martha shook her head. "We're not exotic. I think you'll find yourself disappointed. The sort of stories that sell newspapers," Martha waved her hand like the idea was nonsensical, "you won't find it here. Like I said, not much excitement."

"Well, excitement is subjective," Arden ventured.

"Is it?" The older woman raised her eyebrow, then turned

around to shut off the espresso maker. She pulled down a clear container of something flaky and got out a bottle of milk.

"Muesli," she said. "Locally made, of course. I've got yogurt too, if you don't care for milk."

"No, this is fine," Arden said, though for the life of her she couldn't think of what exactly muesli was, or if she'd ever had it.

She was given a bowl so charmingly uneven it had to have been handmade and a metal spoon with a curved handle.

"Serve yourself," Martha said. "How do you take your coffee?"

"Anyway I can," Arden joked. And when that got no reaction, she added, "Black's fine."

Martha poured her some, wrapping the espresso maker's handle with a kitchen towel, and slid the mug over. Arden took a sip. The brew was slap-in-the-face strong, almost like a test of her fortitude. Just in case, Arden took another sip, making sure not to cringe.

"Watch this," Martha said conspiratorially. Using her fingers, she began a silent countdown.

By the time she reached nine, Ronan descended from his bedroom.

"Mmm, smells good."

"He'd sleep through an atomic bomb but wake up to the smell of coffee." Martha grinned, but what stood out to Arden was the warm affection in the woman's voice. What was that? Love? Devotion? Was she the Mrs. Danvers to his Rebecca? The Alfred to his Bruce Wayne?

"Good morning, Arden. How did you sleep?"

He did look good first thing in the morning. Perfectly rumpled yet effortlessly handsome. His smile broad, sincere.

He wore plaid pajama bottoms and a plain white T-shirt. Feet bare. Hair tussled by sleep.

Arden pushed down a familiar stirring in the pit of her stomach. Most people kept fear where she hid desire.

"I slept okay," she said, forcing her gaze away, toward her food. "There was a noise."

"What noise?" He finger combed his hair back, absentmindedly, smiling still. "I can't possibly be snoring that loudly."

"It was something different," Martha cut in briskly. "Terry and Jacob went to check it out."

"Well, then, we shall know soon enough." He clapped his hands together. "One advantage of living somewhere small."

"With a cell tower, you could know in real time," Arden pointed out, covering her mouth. The muesli was hearty and chewy. It tasted like something that was good for you as opposed to actually tasting good.

"But then there'd be no mystery." Ronan laughed, taking a cup of coffee from Martha. "No suspense."

"It's about knowledge," she persisted.

"I think you're confusing knowledge with information. A popular mistake, but the two are categorically not the same." Ronan took a sip of his coffee with an appreciative "Ah."

"Define it for me then," Arden said, feeling herself switch automatically into journalist mode.

Ronan savored another sip. "Knowledge is information processed. If information is beans, knowledge is coffee." He toasted her with his cup, one eyebrow raised playfully. On paper, he'd sound pedantic in that moment, she thought, but in reality, he was anything but. You could tell he viewed conversations as games, not battles.

She inclined her head to encourage him to say more, but he

seemed absolutely content to leave it at that, utterly absorbed by the enjoyment of the coffee in his cup, the morning, the moment.

Arden spooned some more muesli into her mouth. Soggy with milk now, and still far from a personal favorite, it was rather like eating a weird cardboard-y version of granola.

"I used to never drink this, you know," he said finally. "I was a total hot chocolate fiend. Just goes to show you that people can change."

"Oh, I don't know. I was always a coffee nut."

"Well, change comes in all sorts of ways," he said, offering another gnomic phrase.

Martha looked up at him from perusing a serious-looking ledger.

"We need to go over the agricultural data when you're done," she said to Ronan.

"Of course, but later." He winked at Arden. "First, pancakes."

"What?"

"Don't bother lying to me about how much you're into the muesli. Think of this as me trying to make a good impression."

He set about getting the ingredients and mixing them together.

Ronan Bard was making her pancakes, Arden mused. In his pajamas, no less. Ronan Bard had winked at her. How perfectly surreal. If not for Martha gargoyling over the scene, this could have been a perfect morning after, something straight out of a rom-com.

"Martha, will you be joining us?" he asked, flipping the pancakes expertly with a red silicone spatula.

"I'll just pop into the office for . . ." She seemed to have remembered that the office was a guestroom now. "I'll sit outside for a bit with these figures."

"Are you sure? I'm making the Austrian kind."

She smiled tightly and stepped outside, closing the door softly behind her.

"I know I should be using my time more productively," Ronan said, getting out a pair of plates. "But I've always believed in breakfast being the most important meal of the day."

"Ah."

"I try to eat it at least once or twice a day." He grinned.

And then what? Arden thought. *You work out like a fiend? Or do you just have one of those bodies, one of those metabolisms?*

The "Austrian kind" turned out to be the pancake equivalent of scrambled eggs. With raisins. And perfectly delicious.

Arden complimented the chef. The chef accepted the compliment gracefully, confessing, "It's one of the few things I can actually make."

"How did you learn? Were your parents big cooks?"

He gave her an amused look and shook his head. "I lived in Vienna for a while."

"When?"

"Before here, after Trex."

"That's rather vague," she told him, helping herself to more pancake pieces.

He paused for a moment and looked at her. "You're right. It's just that everything in my life feels like it's separated into eras. There's Trex, and then there's the island. And everything else was either before or after."

"Except that there's nothing after the island, is there?"

He shook his head again, smiling.

"Do you think there will ever be?"

"I can't predict the future, Arden," he said softly. This close she could see every fine line on his face. Not wrinkles, but ghosts of them, revealing the man he would become in time. Here was someone who squinted at the sun and laughed generously. The lines were nothing but reflections of that. Not like the worry lines that had started etching across her forehead over the last few years. Arden thought she could trace every single one of them to a fight, a disappointment, a heartbreak.

Maybe there was something here on the island that kept people looking younger. Like those places in Greece or Japan where everyone lived past a hundred.

She willed herself to focus. "Didn't Trex try to do exactly that? Predict the future?"

"Ah, yes." He laughed mock-ruefully. "A folly of youth, I'm afraid."

"Follies don't sell for billions of dollars," she countered, well in her element now. "Trex technology is still considered revolutionary. Its predictive algorithms are used to this day in—"

Ronan waved his hand, not dismissively, more bashfully. "Come on, that's all . . . it isn't real."

"How so?"

"Not like me, like you, like these pancakes." He grinned. "It's just ones and zeroes and confirmation bias."

"You don't really believe that, do you?"

Ronan scratched his chin. She couldn't tell if the stubble there was blond or gray. Chris's whiskers came in salt-and-peppery despite his hair being black with nary a strand of gray. A follicular mystery.

"What would you like to hear, Arden? Don't say 'the truth.' No one really wants that. But I'd be happy to give you a quippy sound bite to sell your article."

He did cynicism well—just lightly enough to avoid patronizing and with a pleasantly self-deprecating undertone.

She put down her fork. "And what if I actually do want the truth?"

"Oh," he said almost sadly. "That's a tough row to hoe."

Arden smiled. "I didn't think anyone still said that."

"Well, out here, we actually have rows to hoe, so . . ." He smiled back.

"You're avoiding the question."

"No, I'm stalling to give myself time to think of something clever to say."

"You don't strike me as someone who needs time to come up with words."

Ronan took a sip of his coffee. "That was a compliment, wasn't it? I couldn't quite tell."

She noncommittally raised one corner of her mouth. The pancakes, like most comfort foods, were making her sleepy, but with Ronan, she felt she had to be on her toes. She drank some of her coffee. It tasted even harsher tepid.

"I've seen some of your old interviews," she told him. He was fascinating even before the island, so much more than a stereotypical tech bro. There was a restlessness about him, a peculiar combination of brashness and reticence. Such confidence for someone so young, but also allowance for uncertainty, especially in later years.

Everyone knew Ronan's story. It was so quintessentially all-American: a boy from the wrong side of the tracks who pulled himself up by his bootstraps straight into the tech world. His first app, invented by twenty-one and sold a year later, changed social media by introducing more intuitive algorithms. His second app revolutionized the way the world worked. It made him a billionaire several times over well before thirty.

Then there were the lost years of traveling and soul-searching. And then, of course, the island.

It wasn't just that he was viciously smart or ridiculously photogenic. Ronan Bard was genuinely interesting. People clamored to know what he might do next. For someone who'd made a career out of refining predictability, Ronan continued to surprise. You never knew what to expect from him. And certainly, no one had ever expected the island.

"I come across like a bit of an ass in those, don't I?" He pushed his hair back.

"No," Arden replied honestly. "You seem like . . ." She searched for the right words. "Like someone who knows more than he's saying."

"Ah." He held up a pointer finger. "That's the best way to be."

"But you agreed to this interview. After years of silence. Why?"

Ronan pushed some pancake on his plate for a moment, then looked up at her, ready to speak.

Martha came in, without bothering to knock. She wore a serious expression but that was probably just her resting face.

"Ronan, a word," she said in a clipped tone.

He shrugged apologetically, wiped his lips with a napkin, excused himself, and followed her out. Saved by the Martha-shaped bell.

Arden would remember exactly where they left off. She was no good with birthdays or anniversaries, but when it came to interviews, her mind was like a recorder. Why would a man who had stayed away from the public eye as long as Ronan Bard grant an interview request? If she had reception, she could ask the Trex-based app on her phone. It had been known to make surprisingly accurate predictions even if Ronan claimed otherwise. She finished her food while she waited, her mind spinning and spinning, trying to figure out what they were talking about. Perhaps Martha was simply trying to exert some control over the situation. Arden knew the woman didn't want her there.

Or perhaps it was about something else entirely. Maybe that early morning noise. Arden had managed to stop thinking about it completely, but now it was on her mind again.

For all of Ronan's secrets, she was sure this would be the one he wouldn't mind sharing. After all, it affected her too. She was here on the island until the next boat—or until she got her story.

CHAPTER 4.
JACOB.

"WHAT IS IT THEN?"

Terry scratched his head. "It definitely came from up there," he said, thoughtfully jabbing his meaty thumb at the sky. "Maybe it's a small asteroid or something."

Jacob felt a strange pull to go closer and look; at the same time, a part of him wanted nothing more than to take off running in the other direction. Curiosity and fear, the perpetual engines of humanity. He tried thinking about it logically.

Despite its perfectly innocuous appearance, the object disturbed him on a profoundly visceral level. It glowed like an angry eye. Could he be projecting? Would any object like that look out of place in these serene woods, on this peaceful island?

"Janice might know," he said as the thought came to him. "We should go get Janice."

"Oh, yeah," Terry seconded, visibly relieved. "Good idea."

Janice Mann was a former NASA scientist turned archivist. Back on the mainland, all she ever wanted to do was go to space, but the tests grounded her. She turned to the research side of things instead. As she put it, she "kept hitting the glass ceiling so hard and so often it resulted in a permanent concussion." She made pun after pun, saying things like how despite her last name, she wasn't man enough for space after all. There was a level of bitterness, or maybe sadness, beneath the tough, jocular exterior, Jacob thought, but she hid it well—better than most.

As far as he could tell, people did not come to the island because things on the mainland were going swimmingly for them. You had to get properly crushed by the vagaries of life to be willing to leave it all behind and start over somewhere new, to remake yourself into someone new.

But surely Janice had retained enough of her old self to sort out this space debris situation. She was one of the first people that Jacob—or any newcomer—met upon arriving on the island. He still remembered all the questions she asked.

"It's like you're gearing up to write a book about me," he joked.

"A book about everyone," she answered in all seriousness. "A chronicle of the island."

"Why?" he asked.

"For posterity," she replied. "Just in case."

"Just in case of what?" Jacob wanted to ask but didn't. In time, he'd come to understand it. Just in case this grand experiment of free living didn't work out. They were cautious. Realistic.

He liked that. It was something he could trust. Cults and communes that made it into the news—universally for terrible reasons—always seemed to have been started or joined or both with wide-eyed optimism and rampant hopefulness. Cute, but no way to live a life.

"So, we just go back?" Terry said, shuffling from foot to foot.

"I guess." Jacob shrugged. "Something has to be done about all the trees, too. I mean, look at this mess."

If the object was a pupil of the eye, the trees fanned it like eyelashes. It was hard to imagine something so small could cause so much damage, but it wasn't about the size of the thing, Jacob knew, but the velocity of its descent.

Terry took a step toward it. Then another. There was an odd look on his face.

"Hey, man, what are you doing?"

Terry didn't seem to hear him, so Jacob spoke up, "Terry." Then in a near shout, "Terry!"

The big man snapped out of it, like a sleepwalker coming to. He took a step back, frowning. "This thing, it's like it's . . ."

"What?"

Terry chewed his lip. "Calling me?"

"That's just your natural curiosity," Jacob said with no strength of conviction behind his words. "Let's go, man."

It was more than curiosity. Jacob could feel its pull too as they walked away. That thing didn't want to be left behind. No, that made no sense. Jacob shook his head.

During the worst of it, back on the mainland, when mixing and matching his poisons backfired, he'd had some strange trips. Highs where inanimate objects became animate and vice versa. He broke a TV once, convinced it was there to record and play back his life. It was only a few years old, 50" flat screen, crystal clear. And oh so easily breakable.

Funny how technology got more and more fragile as it progressed. Picking up and breaking an old school large screen TV would have taken someone Terry's size, at least.

Ronan sometimes talked about it. The evil ways of consumerism, the built-in obsolescence, the impermanent flimsiness of everyday things. All part of the grand design to keep people in their cages, running on their treadmills, going nowhere.

In principle, Jacob agreed. Right now, he'd be happy to have his phone, though. He'd photograph the glowing object, do an image search, Google it, something.

They'd have to settle for a verbal description. Facts only, none of the emotionally peculiar first impressions.

The walk back felt longer with neither of them talking much. There was a tense network of unspoken words between them; each man held back his unease and put up a false front of nonchalance. It was sobering to realize that even here such posturing remained, that some vestiges of social conditioning proved impossible to shake.

Janice Mann lived in a small wood-clad house with a tall chimney. She tinkered with woodworking in her spare time, and the evidence abounded, from the bench outside to all the bookcases that lined the walls of her home. Her companion of choice was Jupiter, shortened to Jupi—a large, friendly mutt with shaggy fur and a graying snout.

They went to Janice's straight after stopping by at Ronan's to offer an update. They found Martha outside, pacing, her thinking face on.

Why wasn't she inside? Jacob thought. And then he remembered—the journalist. He couldn't imagine Martha being fully on board with that no matter what she said.

Jacob wasn't sure how he felt about it himself. Ronan spoke about it openly at their most recent makeshift town hall meeting.

"I think my prime objective here is to clear away the cobwebs of misconception about our community," he said in front of everybody. "I'd love to say that perception is irrelevant. It should be. But it isn't. And I would be lying if I said I didn't want our message to reach farther in the world. We have accomplished magnificent things in our time here, setting beautiful standards for meaningful living, while things out there," he gestured to the land beyond the ocean, "have only gotten worse." He paused and looked around. "I have no desire to throw our gates open to just anyone. I remain fully committed to keeping our numbers low and our population hand chosen and dedicated. Immigration is the scourge of modern society. It has reshaped most nation's politics and never for the better. We will not repeat the mistakes of the world at large. But our message should be out there. People should know their options and be made aware of the possibilities." Ronan took a sip of water and brushed back his hair with his fingers.

"If we can inspire even a few to start their own meaningful communities, to break away from the suffocating norm and find a better way of life, then I think we ought to. I think that perhaps it is our moral imperative to do so. And I believe we can start with something small, like granting an interview, like showing people who we are and what we are about.

"You mustn't worry. Your privacy will be fully protected. I shall retain the final right of approval for the article, photos, etc. This isn't in any way a betrayal of our principles, merely an expansion upon them. I've never wanted a pulpit, I've never wanted to proselytize. Well, maybe once or twice."

This got Ronan a laugh.

"I suppose this is the easiest or even laziest way I could think of about how to tell the world about us, our values, our beliefs. If it doesn't work, if it falls on deaf ears—as it very well might—I will be the first to admit it. But I think it's worth a try. What say you?"

There was a vote. The majority, unsurprisingly, had sided with Ronan. And that was that.

Jacob had voted for Ronan's idea too. He liked the sound of "moral imperative," though he'd never thought of himself as a particularly moral man. This seemed like a good deed handed to him on a platter. Who knows? What if the journalist wrote an article that inspired other people to start communities like theirs?

Was it even possible? Wouldn't they need to have Ronan's sort of money? Jacob couldn't imagine there were a lot of benevolent billionaires out there.

His first impression of Ronan Bard, before he had ever met the man, back when he was only a figure in the news, was that of yet another arrogant upstart. Young, good looking, obscenely wealthy, Ronan was easy to resent. But Jacob had never given the man much thought until he heard him speak at that famous TED Talk.

Not once in his life had Jacob ever heard a single speech by anyone that had resonated with him so deeply. It was revelatory to have your personal thoughts and feelings laid out so precisely and eloquently. It was so validating.

He'd watched it so many times he could quote parts of it by heart.

"Our country has failed us. Our politicians have failed us. The American Dream is dead. The media and the pundits are distracting us with fake news and meaningless trivialities to keep us from seeing the truth. The standard of living in the US is lower than in any other first-world country. Pick an important topic: life expectancy, gender and pay equality, voting rights, education, crime, homelessness. This country is failing in every single way. The golden promise of it has been eroded, revealing nothing but gilt. Instead of learning from our history, we find ways to bury it.

Instead of speaking about what matters, we obsess over TikTok. We don't know the faces and platforms of our leaders, but we spend hours watching social media celebrities doing and talking about nothing. As a society, we have become dumber and more complacent, and we have been encouraged to do that at every turn by the powers that be. Stupid people are the easiest to lead. We play video games and shop, while the world gets lit on fire, while it slips beneath the waves, while it becomes increasingly uglier and more hostile. We waste our lives working jobs we hate toward an uncertain retirement. We cycle through meaningless diversions while our freedoms are slowly stripped away from us. We are sleepwalking."

The expression in Ronan's eyes, that dramatic pause, never failed to send shivers down Jacob's spine. It was all so . . . true. The final part rang truest.

"Well, I'm here to say, wake up. Look around. Walk away. There is another path."

Ronan's speech had branded him anything from a lunatic to a messiah. He took it all in stride. He calmly explained what he meant by another path, and that was that.

It was up to the interested individuals to seek him out. Jacob tried to forget about it, but complacency was harder to succumb to once someone succeeded in calling you out on it. Willful ignorance was no longer an option. Jacob thought of nothing else for a long time. Then he surrendered, and he reached out to Ronan Bard.

The rest was paperwork, logistics, an elaborate prescreening process, gut-churning worrying and waiting to hear if he had been approved. Once he got that life-changing "yes," the rest was easy—mere planning and practical matters. Downsizing decades of life to suitcases, paring down to essentials. Jacob was amazed to realize how much of what he owned he did not need. Books he would never reread, or get around to reading in the first place. Clothes he didn't wear. Gifts he never needed but had no heart to throw out.

Jacob placed it all in open boxes and set them outside on the curb. Then from his apartment window, he watched people walk by and peruse his trash, looking for treasures. One by one, they came and took his things away; the strangers dismantled one life so he could be free to build another.

He wouldn't miss any of it: the city's cacophony of sirens, car horns, and angry shouts finding him through the open window. He wouldn't miss any of it, he knew, as he handed in his resignation at work. As he longingly eyed his collection of benzos and booze, he was all too aware he'd miss some of what those brought him.

He couldn't bring it to the island. Ronan had made it clear that he was happy to help him get and stay clean, but any slipup would send him right back to the mainland.

"I don't believe in three strikes," Ronan explained, his voice firm but not unkind. "We're not a sports team or middle school. Adults should own their responsibilities and atone for their transgressions as they occur. We're trying to be better, all of us. This is how we start."

And Jacob, having for the first time found the thing he wanted more than a quick oblivion, agreed. He put his alcohol in a bag and took it to the local park with a heavy homeless population, though afterward he questioned that choice. The rest of his little helpers he threw down the kitchen sink drain, running the garbage disposal for good measure.

He arrived on the island in a state of permanent jitteriness, unsettled by the monumental changes and battling a low-grade withdrawal. Ronan was right. There were people here who could help him. Former addiction counselors, even psychologists. Jacob figured he couldn't be the only one with chemical dependencies looking for a fresh start. Yet he was made to feel like the only one in the best possible way. A private space, private therapy sessions, all while he was slowly integrating into the community, doing his bit to make it a better place.

No more paper pushing, no more juggling meaningless numbers. He went back to doing the thing he had learned to do in his father's garage: dirty, honest work to fix broken things. It felt more than right—it felt symbolic.

Every community needed a mechanic. What he couldn't fix, he'd read up on. He even occasionally watched YouTube videos at Ronan's if a particularly recalcitrant piece of damaged equipment came his way. The bright world of each video, with their endless commercials, upset Jacob. It was a strange scab-picking feeling, like seeing your ex out and about, uncomfortably revisiting a remnant of a life left behind. He restricted himself to written manuals only. Fortunately, there was no shortage of those on the island. There was an amazingly well-stocked private library. And Janice had her own collection, too.

The sunlight found his eyes, making him flinch reflexively. It returned him back to reality.

"So, what was it?" Martha demanded upon seeing them.

"No idea," Terry offered unhelpfully.

She pursed her lips impatiently.

"It's something from the sky, like an asteroid or a meteorite." Jacob stepped in to explain. "It leveled a bunch of trees out there. We were going to get Janice to take a look at it."

"Oh," Martha said. "Yes, that's a good idea. Come straight back with her afterward, will you?"

Janice was outside chopping wood, neat, methodical chops, one after another. She had short hair shot through with gray and a no-nonsense demeanor to rival Martha's, yet with a notable undercurrent of warmth and humor. Small, just over five feet, and wiry, her build and energy were more suitable for someone decades younger. If Jacob had to guess, he'd place Janice in her late fifties. It didn't really matter, though; age didn't mean much on the island. Jupi walked lazy circles around her, but he paused to welcome the visitors, his tail wagging excitedly.

"Fellas," she greeted them.

"Janice."

Jacob was good with a nod, but Terry reached down to hug her, enveloping the small woman with his huge arms. Jacob petted Jupi's fuzzy head.

"What's up?" Janice asked, once released from Terry's affections. "Need a book or something?"

"Your expertise, actually," Jacob told her. "We found something."

"Something like . . . ?" she narrowed her eyes, highlighting the wrinkles in the corners.

"A space ball," Terry said with a laugh.

"Would it have anything to do with the hellacious noise that woke me up out of a perfectly pleasant dream this morning?"

Jacob clapped his hands. "That's the one."

"Let me change my shoes."

She reemerged, having switched her rubber boots for hiking boots and adding a rucksack on her back. Jupi did an excited loop, sensing adventure.

"Lead the way," Janice said.

CHAPTER 5.
MARTHA.

SHE HAD NEVER placed too much value on intuition. Her mother, while trying to make sense of the world, got into psychics and crystal balls and mysterious energies of the universe—all the things her father, the parent Martha was always closest to, had always dismissed as hippie crap. It left Martha with a perpetual skepticism verging on scorn when it came to anything other than factual matters. Yet upon hearing the words "something from the sky," she felt a distinctly unpleasant, vertiginous shift in her stomach—like things were about to change, and she wasn't going to like it. There was that niggling sense of alarm.

She took a deep breath, counted to five, and let it out. It was the only advice her mother gave her that actually worked. There was nothing to worry about, she told herself, repeating the breathing exercise. Objects fell from space sometimes. It happened. Debris was everywhere. The world was a messy place. As above so below. All that.

They'd deal with it the way they always had: as a community of reasonable people. As a proper democracy.

It was, after all, one of the main draws to Ronan's rhetoric for her. The way the man disparaged the state of American democracy resonated strongly within her. The two of them were similarly disillusioned.

"America," Ronan had said in his now-famous TED Talk, and on other platforms of the time, "is no longer a democracy. It is a country that stopped listening to its people. The politicians do not elect leaders based on popular votes. They enact laws that most citizens do not support. The system has become self-serving, petty, and fractured. The dream is dead."

Ronan's words were everywhere for a while, setting public discourse on fire. He was lauded and condemned. "A Pretty-Boy Prophet," the headlines screamed, their words steeped in condescension. He was easy to dismiss, with his youth, his looks, his money. Easy to love, but easier to hate. And hatred had always been the simpler choice for the crowds. Their hands were all too willing to reach for pitchforks.

Ronan had confided in her later about the death threats he received.

"Were you scared?" she asked him.

He rubbed the back of his neck, an endearingly boyish gesture he used to stall for time. "I think I kind of felt invincible at the time," he said finally. "Like I had my mission, and I was meant to see it through."

And, of course, he did.

The island was a beautiful vision materialized, and its location a secret kept surprisingly well. With a climate mild enough to sustain a happy existence—Ronan modeled a lot of his ideas on places like Finland and Iceland but couldn't imagine happiness with so much winter and darkness—and the soil fertile enough to support most agricultural efforts, and views beautiful enough to make you never long for anywhere else, it couldn't have been more perfectly chosen.

Ronan had scouted location after location until he found this one: his paradise on Earth. His new Eden. For all the nicknames, most still referred to it as just "the island." It sufficed.

A dream made real, it had come to feel so stable, so permanent, and yet something in Martha's gut asked her now if this too could be destroyed like every other paradise throughout time.

She shivered and crossed her arms. All she wanted to do was go inside and talk to Ronan about it. Actually, what she wanted to do first was send that journalist woman away, back to where she came from.

Martha didn't think too highly of her ilk. And in person, Arden had done nothing to dispel her suspicions.

What were the odds of Arden being committed to helping Ronan spread his word? What if all she was looking for was an angle, a prodding fingernail trying to peel off the label so that she could rewrite her own contents? Who wanted the truth when you could sell a scandal?

Ronan could get carried away, Martha knew. Not all of his ideas were popular—the immigration thing alone—and a lot of them could be easily misinterpreted by someone determined to do so and spun into something ugly. She should be there with him, she decided. Or he should be out here with her. They should be talking about the object in the woods, whatever it was. She needed to concentrate on what was important, no matter how unpalatable she found that Arden woman with her polished good looks and professional slickness.

One last deep breath, and Martha let herself back into the

house. It smelled like pancakes and coziness. She wondered how much was said.

"Ronan, a word?"

He had the good grace to not keep her waiting. With a nod and an excuse, he followed her out.

"What's going on?" he asked as he took a look around and stretched. "Ah, nice morning."

"That thing in the woods, the one that made the noise."

"Yes?" He stopped admiring the skies and snapped to attention.

"It seems to have come from outer space, according to Terry and Jacob. They are getting Janice to take a look at it. Apparently it leveled part of the woods."

"Janice. Yes, good idea. Just think, something from the skies." Ronan's eyes lit up like a kid. "Our very own piece of the cosmos."

Always the dreamer. Martha loved that about him. Still, she worried.

"If that's what it is, should it be reported?" she said. "Wouldn't people have to come here to study it?"

"Oh, no." Ronan waved the notion off. "No one has to know if we don't want them to. It can be our very own space rock."

Did he ever worry at all? Like her? Like the rest of mere mortals? Was that how he kept his brow so smooth all these years, while the rest got wrinkles and creases?

She sometimes felt the irrepressible buoyancy of him nudging her own gravity, making her lighter on her feet. She relished the sensation as a break from herself.

"How's the interview going?" Martha pivoted.

"Oh, we're just having pancakes right now. I made Kaiserschmarrn. Didn't presoak the raisins in rum but it still came out very well."

"I'm serious, Ronan." Martha raised her eyebrows, then furrowed them. "She's an outsider. A stranger."

"As we all were once." A beatific smile underscored his words.

He could be so infuriating, but she could never properly get or stay mad at him. Ronan was just so . . . Ronan.

He seemed to sense her mood. A smile gave way to a more somber expression as he studied her face thoughtfully. "What are you concerned about really?"

"I don't want your message to get misinterpreted," she responded with a half-truth.

"I've been misinterpreted before," he said. "A lot. It doesn't matter. You can't please everyone, and only a fool would try."

Martha watched a small procession of ants cross the patch of land between them— committed and purpose-driven—ignoring the feet of giants next to them the way humans ignored the mountains, because we were accustomed to navigating around: all things everyone took for granted.

Martha raised her eyes. "I don't trust her," she said, her voice quiet but resolute.

"You've made that abundantly clear when you cleaned the office out of every single piece of paper," Ronan replied teasingly, his smile returning. "Come on. It's okay. I know what I'm doing. You trust me, right?"

"Of course."

He put a hand on Martha's shoulder and gave it an affectionate squeeze. It was what passed for intimacy between them, and it suited them both.

"I should get back inside before Arden steals all our top secrets," Ronan joked. "Or at least my top pancake recipes."

Martha indulged him with a half smile.

"You coming?"

She got the impression he wanted her to say no. It wasn't anything in his voice. Perhaps she was projecting. What if he simply wanted to enjoy the company of a young, attractive stranger without supervision?

"I better get on with my morning," Martha replied tactfully. "Things to do, people to see. I'll circle back by the time the guys get back with Janice."

"Have fun," he said.

"And you. Just not too much."

Ronan winked and went back in, leaving Martha alone outside. Just her and the ants. She felt ridiculous. Very much like a school principal. How did one practice discipline without coming across as a disciplinarian? Was such a thing even possible?

Martha sighed and started walking. There were a few people she was thinking of stopping by to see. Strange to think that for most of her life, these appointments would be done over the phone or virtually. There was an unparalleled difference in doing everything in person. Besides, this way she was able to get her steps in.

Martha had never been thin, not when it was in fashion, and not when people stopped caring about it, proclaiming big to be beautiful. She was never fat either, despite what some of the crueler comments at her former work claimed. She was stout, solidly built, and had more than enough time to become accustomed to it. But it was only after she came to live on the island that she began to feel fit for the first time. All that time outside, all that walking.

It was a pleasant feeling of strength in her limbs and stamina in her spirit—tangible proof of Ronan's way of life being better.

There were fitness classes, though she never attended any. And yoga classes, which she tried and didn't much care for. It seemed to her that walking alone was enough exercise if done sufficiently, and so she tried to do so daily.

Martha had never walked much back on the mainland. She drove or, in a pinch, took public transportation. The city felt hostile with its endless construction, traffic, and noise. Once someone tried to snatch her purse. She felt a tug on it, and it took a moment to realize it was deliberate. The street was so busy with after-work pedestrians. She tugged back, meeting eyes with a thin man, all sharp cheekbones and heavy stubble. He growled at her, a distinctly unsettling thing. She blanched, but recovered quickly, opening her mouth as if to scream, and he bolted, disappearing into the crowd.

An unremarkable experience by city standards, but it got to her. She dreamed of the thin man with his dark, narrow eyes for months to come.

She didn't get harassed much in other ways for there was no better protection for a woman than plainness. It rendered one invisible in a crowd as surely as any magic cloak.

She'd go to art galleries, museums, or book readings, unwilling to deny herself culture just because she didn't have anyone to go with. No one had ever noticed her at those events. Even the bartenders took a while to zero in on her if she tried to order a drink. Then there was Ronan. Ronan saw her. That first time and ever since.

Here, on the island, Martha was very much a visible person. Somebody, at last. And it was nice; she enjoyed it to an extent. She wondered what the others made of her, though. As Ronan's right hand, she enjoyed a certain degree of power or at least responsibility. But without Ronan's innate charm, there was nothing to mitigate the position's sharper edges.

Fortunately, it had seldom, if ever, been an issue. They did not play good cop, bad cop. All decisions were made democratically and carried out multilaterally. A joint effort each time.

Every so often, a nagging thought darkened the threshold of Martha's mind. What if something happened to Ronan? Would she, as his successor, be able to continue carrying out his vision? Or would their perfect world slowly fall apart?

It was hardly meant to last, after all. Not enough people, not enough children. It seemed to her like one of those obscure religious movements that died out as their members did.

Martha read a book about Shakers once: doomed by celibacy, among other things. Not enough converts to sustain it. Another utopia that went bust despite best intentions.

She read things like that to be practical, to keep her heart on an even keel. Yet deep down, each time she was done with a book, a small secret joy warmed her from the inside—a thought that what they had here on the island was different. Better.

What they had created was above the faults and flaws of other failed Edens.

No extreme ideas, no wacky ideology, or unsustainable beliefs. Only reason, only better angels. Ronan offered hope as generously as a safety net. All he asked for in return was for people to be good, to themselves and to each other. A small cost, really.

And then, there were days when Martha thought, *So what if this cannot be sustained?* Even if it were to collapse after Ronan, it still would have mattered. It would forever be something to reflect upon with wonder and know that you were a part of something special, something pure.

Ronan hadn't made any active effort to expand or ensure longevity of the island's dream in a long time. Not until now. There was almost something admirable in his "after me, the flood" attitude. Martha wished to think the same.

Turning her mind to practical matters, she thought of the felled wood and realized she'd need to notify the lumberjack crew at the very least—unless Terry and Jacob would think to do it. They probably would even without her telling them. They were smart, considerate people. Martha had always struggled to rein in her tendency to micromanage, and this was an excellent example of when to pull back. Perhaps she should instead go speak with their lead agriculturalist, Agnes Kay, to see what could be done about the injured plot of land.

Agnes, who was almost her contemporary, had been a respected professor and an award-winning author back in the day. Though she got fired and disgraced after having an affair with one of her undergrads. They were both of legal age, stayed together, and got married, but the fine details got lost in the puritanical fist shaking of the powers that be. Agnes was eager to come to the island—her husband less so—but he had adjusted well enough since.

But first she needed something to jump start her blood sugar, and she knew just the thing.

Having a plan put a spring in her step. Everything was solvable, she told herself. They'd deal with the space rock, Arden would leave, and life would get back to normal.

The morning sun had found Martha's face as if in agreement. Together, they proceeded to seize the day.

CHAPTER 6.
ARDEN.

ARDEN USED TO date someone obsessed with dystopias. "Why not utopias?" she had asked him once. "Because they are so boring," he replied. "Happy is boring."

Tolstoy, one of her parents' favorites, seemed to agree in his sage estimation of the happy and unhappy family dynamics so much so he made a career out of it.

Yet here on the island, Arden couldn't help but see the attraction of utopia. It was peaceful. More than that, it embodied a word so outside of her quotidian vocabulary she had to dig for it: harmonious.

After Ronan returned to their interrupted breakfast, he and Arden finished their pancakes, and then he offered her a guided tour.

"Of course," she replied.

She believed herself to be too savvy a journalist to fall for presentation tricks. No Potemkin villages or perfect North Korea façades, anyway, the island was too small for any of that. What she saw before her was an authentic community: self-contained and functioning precisely. These people seemed fully engaged with their work and perfectly content with their place in the world.

BEAUTIFUL, ONCE

They didn't have a brainwashed glaze to their expression, didn't wear matching drab clothing, didn't step to the beat of some shared internal drum. There was nothing of a cult here, she realized, with a pang of disappointment. These people seemed genuinely happy. And to contradict her ex, who was a dick anyway, no one looked bored.

Ronan, playing the perfect host, introduced her around town, inquiring if anyone would be amenable to answer a few questions. Arden had more than a few to ask, all too aware that each person here had their own story, an entire life abandoned in favor of trying on a new one.

It was a one-size-fits-all version of the American dream. People from different walks of life and social stratospheres came together to engage in Ronan's vision of something better. They had abandoned their complicated jobs back home, mortgages, and families—all for this.

"Do you know what a hedge fund managing consultant does?" the stoop-shouldered man in his late forties asked her. His name was Truman Larsen, but he went by Tru. Clad in denim overalls and a floppy beige hat, he was tending to a hydroponic vertical garden and seemed to enjoy answering questions with questions.

"I have a vague idea," she replied.

"You're ahead of the curve then, aren't you? Most people don't. And who could blame them? It isn't a real job. And if what you do isn't real, then what are you?"

"And what are you now?" Arden tilted her head.

"What do you think?" He beamed, gesturing to his creation proudly.

"A gardener?" Arden ventured.

"A hydroponics expert," Tru exclaimed, his smile increasing in wattage.

"I'm not sure I know more about hydroponics than I do about hedge funds," she said, using an old trick of downplaying her intelligence to get the subject to say more.

"Hydroponics are the future of agriculture," Tru explained eagerly. No more questions for answers, only declarative sentences for him. "It's a science of growing things indoors or in small spaces without soil and with only a minimal amount of water."

"So how do things grow without soil and water? I kind of thought those were prerequisites."

Tru held up a pointy index finger. "That's where the science comes in. You use water-based mineral nutrient solutions. You can go organic, inorganic, hybrid. Though we wouldn't do inorganic here, of course."

"What works as an organic nutrient?" Arden asked. It was all interesting enough but by and large irrelevant to the story she wanted to tell. Still, she had to start somewhere. If Ronan brought her here, this was obviously something he wanted her to see and know about. He was in the corner at present, checking on something green that looked remarkably like cannabis.

Tru rubbed his hands together. "Fish excrement, duck manure, you'd be amazed."

Arden sketched a fish and a duck in her notepad along with a doodle of a steaming pile of poo.

"But surely there's no shortage of land here," she posited, gesturing to the island at large. "Or water."

Tru bounced up and down on the balls of his feet as if he had anticipated the question and had a doozy of a reply locked, loaded, and ready to go.

"That's the mistake people often make, confusing the present with the future, allowing the plenty of now to serve as an excuse not to prepare for what's next. Water and land shortages will be a huge problem the world over in the years to come. Especially, the kind you need to grow things. We are just getting an early start, getting ready."

"Always be prepared," she quipped.

"Exactly." Tru flashed her a Boy Scout salute. "Now, do you want to try something?"

"Sure," she said, turning briefly to Ronan. Their eyes met, and he winked.

When she turned back, Tru was handing her a perfectly ripe medium-sized tomato. She took it from him.

"It's lovely."

"Try it, would you?"

Arden ate tomatoes in salads, washed and sliced. For all she knew this thing had just come off the vine. There wasn't a knife in sight. When in Rome: She rubbed at it with her palm, brought it to her mouth, and took a bite as if it were an apple.

Freshness burst across her taste buds. It *was* lovely. Perfect, in fact. As far as tomatoes went, anyway. She told Tru as much, causing the man's unshaven face to positively blush.

All compliments aside, Tru seemed reluctant to talk about himself, offering few specifics or emotionally charged tidbits.

"I did everything right," he told her. "Back on the mainland. I checked every box. A lot of us here had, I think you'll find. And it led to nothing but disappointment. It wasn't real, none of it, you see? An illusory prosperity. Money paid to me for services that did nothing but make the rich richer. Money paid to the bank for the illusion of ownership of things I was taught to want. I spent time with people just like me, who bought into the same lie and continued to perpetuate it. We were all trapped in the same cage, running on the same wheels. It was all a joke."

He shook his head with a bemused smile, like he couldn't believe that was his life once.

"How did you come to live here?" Arden asked after a bit.

Tru glanced at Ronan. Arden thought she caught a small, barely perceptible nod exchanged.

"I had done some work for Ronan. Finances. One day we got to talking, and the things he was saying . . . they were just so different." Tru shook his head, raising his eyebrows. "I didn't know what to make of it—of him—at first, but then I found myself thinking about it. Over and over, you know? It got into my head like one of those earworm songs. An intentional community. It just sounded so real."

"And the rest as they say is history," Ronan concluded jocularly, coming up to them. "And it isn't just the tomatoes either," he added, quirking his eyebrow toward the cannabis. There were some cucumbers growing there, too. "All green, all fresh."

She wasn't sure what he was offering and didn't ask. It felt like he was ending her interview with Tru, and Arden felt slightly irritated because she wasn't done.

She threw in one last question: "Are you happy here, Tru? Any regrets?" Two questions, technically.

"What's there to regret?" the stoop-shouldered man said simply, putting his hands in his overall pockets.

They left shortly after, with the taste of fresh tomato still lingering on Arden's lips.

"Hydroponics?" she said, just to say something. Ronan may have perfected the art of casual silences, but she still found them awkward. Rather, she found Ronan's presence too much to take without words stitching up the distance between them.

"Just one of the island's many treats." He smiled. The pants and shirt he wore appeared to be made of some sort of linen fabric. They draped his tall, lean frame perfectly. Arden wouldn't be surprised if they were woven locally. Self-sufficiency was king here.

The sun was out in full now, hot without beating you over the head with it. It offered the sort of warmth that energized you as opposed to leaving you drained.

All the buildings on the island were small, typically one story. Other than that there was no uniformity to the style, design, or color. Each one had a personality all of its own. The streets connecting them were flattened dust. There were no cars on the island, only a variety of bikes: smaller two-wheelers for the general population and larger cargo trikes for businesses.

Arden tried to remember the last time she rode a bike. Was it really in college? She didn't count the stationary one at the gym. It seemed that after her college days she outgrew biking as a mode of transportation. It had become too unwieldy to contend with—the sweaty clothes, the helmet hair. Did anyone on the island even care about things like that?

There was no clear separation between private residences and commercial properties. No strip malls of suburbia. Nothing like that.

Arden wasn't sure of the island's size or the number of people living here, but it had to be small. She could see that. A perfectly arranged, curated society.

She remembered one of Ronan's more famous interviews, having rewatched and reread them all in preparation for this assignment.

"The only way for a society to stay happy is through staying small. It is impossible to maintain shared values in a larger structure. The threads of cohesiveness stretch and tear. Time and again, we see this happen, in the news, in history lessons, and yet most continue to ignore it."

In the interview, Ronan wore a navy blue, slim-fitting suit that set off his eyes perfectly. But his presence forced you to focus on his words, not his appearance.

"Time and again, the happiest countries selected are some of the smallest on Earth. Iceland, Finland. Places where people have forged a strong national character based on shared values. Where they feel supported by their government. Where a true democracy is practiced. Time and again, on the other hand, some of the largest countries in the world fall to autocratic rule. These places experience large levels of unhappiness among its people, which results in making tragic political choices."

"Are you saying that a key to success is as simple as for a nation to stay small?" he was asked.

"No, of course not." Ronan smiled. "That would be terribly reductive. I mean, Greenland isn't particularly happy, and it has less than one hundred thousand people. There are many other factors. But there are undeniable patterns. They show us that the size of a place is hugely significant. That a cultural cohesiveness is hugely significant."

"Does this bring us to your famously controversial views on immigration?" The interviewer adjusted her glasses with a precise gesture. Arden remembered thinking how she wished it were her sitting across from Ronan and asking him all these questions.

Ronan's smile grew wider—a man perfectly at ease with himself. "My views are more on the side of infamous, I'd say," he joked, playing at self-deprecation. "I stand by everything I've said, but I do believe most of it has been taken out of context."

"You don't believe in closed borders?"

"I believe in nations taking care of their own citizens first and foremost," he sidestepped expertly. "Making that a priority."

"What about people who are dying? Who need saving? What about those applying for a political asylum?"

"You can't save everybody," Ronan said simply, and for the first time, Arden wondered if there might be a hint of cruelty behind that perfectly handsome, amicable exterior. "You can't save the world. You have to start locally, take care of your own. You can't offer handouts when your own children are starving, when your own people are homeless."

The interviewer took a sip of water. "What about countries who manage to do both?"

"Not one of them has done it successfully," Ronan parried. "Every country that has tried this has experienced high levels of local discontent, often leading to civil unrest and decisive restructure of government toward the right."

"And how do you explain this?"

"I believe that the general population is nowhere near as charitable by nature as its leaders want it to believe. We are all tribal beings. Over time, we came to conglomerate into larger tribes, but only those woven together by shared bonds stay and thrive. Artificial conglomeration doesn't work. To quote Yeats, 'Things fall apart, the center cannot hold.' It's happened in the Middle East, Africa, in Europe—just look at Yugoslavia. I can give you example after example, but I don't think anyone is interested in that much uncomfortable truth."

Ronan leaned back in his seat and steepled his fingers, looking very much like a misunderstood prophet.

"And why do you think people view your words as uncomfortable truth?" the interviewer asked, pushing up her glasses again.

"Because people don't want to be shown a mirror that exposes them for who they are. People want to be comforted by the convenient lies they believe of themselves and the world. It's easier that way. Easier to think of themselves as charitable and nice and, most importantly, not responsible. Easier to never have to re-examine their own culpability or set of beliefs. Easier to have their facts of life presented as fait accompli. Easier to look away, preferably toward a TV screen with something inane on it, and not give another thought to the state of the world or their place in it."

Arden remembered pausing the video here, rewinding, then rewatching the last bit. Did Ronan Bard really believe all of this strongly enough to risk offending so many? She didn't know whether to admire or despise him for it. But was he wrong? When was the last time she heard a controversial point of view expressed by anyone she knew? People seemed to simply repeat the things from their choice of a news source, dramatically polarized views without a hint of a middle ground.

Ronan looked like someone whose ideas were all his own. A lot of them were conventionally palatable, easy to agree with. Some were radically not. But you had to give it to him—the man thought for himself and didn't pander.

"And your own society, the one on your island," the interviewer went on, "it subscribes to and reflects your views to a T?"

Ronan sat up in his chair. "Nothing is to a T, Alice," he replied, smiling. "Never. Except perhaps a tailor-made suit." He plucked at his own lapel jokingly. "And even that isn't a guarantee."

He took a sip of water.

"I set up a community of like-minded individuals, sure. People as determined to live a purposeful life as I am. But it is wildly unrealistic to never expect a disagreement. We vote on all of our decisions. And unlike most mock democracies of the world, on the island the popular vote wins. Every time."

"But you do allow immigration to your island, in a manner of speaking?"

She's good, Arden thought. *I want to be just like Alice Tanaka someday. Just look at that confidence.*

"We are a community in the making. We allow in carefully prescreened individuals who we believe share our values and can contribute directly to our prosperity."

"You don't think that's a bit narrow-minded?"

Ronan tilted his head to the side as if amused. "Ask me again in a decade when the mainland is on fire, and our island is thriving."

Alice smiled. Their confidence levels matched so impressively, it was like watching Godzilla go against King Kong.

"I'll be sure to do that," Alice said after a moment. And Ronan told her he was looking forward to it, a perfect gentleman to the end.

She never got the chance to, of course. Alice Tanaka was shot and killed by a raving madman at her son's wedding. It was unclear if her killer was raging against Asian Americans, gay people, or Alice and her family in particular. He was gunned down by the arriving police, still foaming at the mouth with hateful rhetoric.

Had Alice lived and gotten her second interview with Ronan, she would have seen that he had made good on his promise. The world was on fire with wars and climate disasters, but out here on his island, in this perfect microcosm, people were happy.

And now she was here, in a place Alice Tanaka would have loved to visit. Arden took a deep breath, marveling at the strangeness of it all, and refocused on her surroundings.

There was a community repair shop, specializing in anything and everything, including, of course, the ubiquitous bicycles. A grocery store was more along the lines of an open market with stalls upon stalls of fruit and vegetables, shelves of baked goods, preserves, and freshly made sides and meals.

She saw a white building with a self-explanatory Rod of Asclepius sign above its doors, it, a library-slash-community meeting hall, a charmingly decorated café which likely doubled as a restaurant and a bar in the evenings.

Everything purpose made. Everything necessary. It was refreshing, really. Back home, Arden lived in a trendy neighborhood, littered with trendy shops. Not a single one of them sold anything anyone might need. It was a strictly want-based system. A proper grocery store was blocks and blocks away, but you could buy obscenely expensive gourmet cheeses right across the street. No library for nearly a mile, but a bougie over-curated bookstore with more style than substance on the next street over.

What values—or absence thereof—did that setup betray? Arden lived there because the buildings were handsome and rich with history, because she liked the sound of her address spoken out loud and what it said about her. Now, she considered it objectively; it seemed so false, all of it.

She shook her head as if to psychically dislodge Ronan from getting inside. This was vacation mentality. You go to some beautiful, tropical island with friendly natives and endless sunshine and warm ocean, and think, "Yes! This is the life." But it isn't real. Only an illusion, a postcard come to life. Sooner or later, you had to get back to the real world.

Still, people lived for vacations, for those brief getaways from reality.

The houses were all standalone, which Arden, the lifelong city dweller, had relished. No shared walls. No neighbors trying your patience.

Guess it didn't matter how community-minded this place was, she mused. There were still boundaries left in place to stay on the safe side.

"Have you ever read Alex Garland's *The Beach*?" Arden ventured. It was one of the few questions on her list she wasn't sure about asking, but how could she not? The comparisons between two island paradises were inevitable.

"I have," Ronan replied with a small smile, letting her know he was onto her. "I've even watched the movie."

"And?"

"And?" he echoed jocularly.

"Surely, you can't ignore the parallels."

"Surely I can," he bantered. "You're talking about what, a few dozen backpackers in huts on the beach living primitive lives, getting high, and scraping by?"

"I'm talking about a small, intentional, utopian community, protective of their land and hostile to outsiders."

"That's a terribly reductive comparison, Arden. Sensationalized but weak. You can do better."

She mused how anyone else would have made that sound combative or patronizing, but with Ronan it simply came across as playful.

She pushed on. "I think the question is whether *you* can do better." Strong, bold, she liked it. "Better than all the rest of the homespun utopias that time and again collapsed onto themselves."

Ronan smiled broadly and spread his arms. "I have nothing to prove to anyone. None of us do. We're just trying to be our best selves living our best lives. You know, all those fun clichés. We're not the place of Garland's imagination. We have technology, contingency plans, strategy."

"But you've built a paradise. Aren't you worried about it being . . . well, lost?"

"Arden, look around."

She did, taking in the endless expanse of blue skies above and blue water all around. She could see how a place like that might wrap you in the safe arms of forever.

Was there fragility beneath the sun-kissed surface here? How could one tell for sure if what they had was a castle or merely a paper drawing of one? The ground under Arden's feet felt as firm as any.

She met his eye, noting how open, how proud of this place he seemed. And if there was something else there for a moment, she could not read it.

"What would you like to see next?" asked Ronan.

"How about the library?"

"As you wish." He gestured *après vous*, and she moved toward the building, after waiting for a bicyclist to pass. The last time she saw this many cyclists—at least as far as the percentage to the general population went—was in Copenhagen. She commented on that to Ronan.

"I love Copenhagen," he told her enthusiastically.

"Then you know of Christiania," she said, congratulating herself on weaving that into the conversation so organically.

"Of course," Ronan admitted, stopping outside the library, sensing the question to come.

Someone had decorated the entrance with two sculptures on either side of the doors, reminiscent of New York Public Library's lions, Patience and Fortitude, only these were two unicorns. Whimsical enough to make you laugh out loud in childlike wonder.

"What do you think of Christiania?" Arden asked, struggling to keep a serious face. "I'm sure you've heard the comparisons."

"I have," Ronan agreed, unconsciously petting one of the unicorns. They were impressively life-sized, or at least horse-sized—since she had no idea about exact unicorn dimensions.

"And?" she prompted.

"And I think it's a lazy and reductive comparison, like most such things, but I admire the dream behind Christiania. Always have. I think it's a crying shame that the real world found a way to bleed through and ruin it."

"All those dealers coming in," Arden said with sympathy.

"The community should have protected themselves better, had stronger security measures in place. But I suppose it's difficult, close to impossible, when you are located in the middle of another city."

"The Vatican City manages," Arden pointed out.

"The Vatican has the Swiss Guard and Gendarmerie Corps," Ronan countered.

"And you?"

"Me?" He raised his eyebrow in amusement.

"What protects you?"

"The ocean." He smiled, gesturing all around. "And additional privacy, bought and paid for."

"If only Oceania had your budget," she said, wondering if she was pushing too far.

"A dream without a budget to back it up is bound to fail," Ronan agreed matter-of-factly. "Now, shall we?"

Inside the library, it was a good ten degrees breezier, though not uncomfortable. It looked like most small-town libraries, which is to say it looked nothing like the city libraries Arden was used to. No messes, no homeless people, no strange odors.

In here, it only smelled of books. A quiet place with shelves upon shelves of bound knowledge.

None of the bookcases quite matched, she noted, adding to the homegrown effect of the place that had expanded organically over time, but the categories were stated clearly and arranged neatly. More importantly, though unsurprisingly, this library was very well stocked.

She complimented Ronan.

"We try," he accepted graciously. "You can judge the place by its library, just as you can judge a person by their book collection, don't you think?"

She agreed, thinking of John Waters' famous quote. Then most of Arden's personal library was on her Kindle, so what did that make her? Difficult to judge, she hoped.

There was a tall, broad-framed woman shelving a bunch of books in the back.

"Oh, hey," she said. "I'm Rhonda. Be right with you."

Far from the stereotypical older, thin, bespectacled, and cardigan-wearing version of a librarian, Rhonda was youngish, robust, and looked like she could wrestle a bull into submission, which, after they got to talking, was indeed one of the many things she used to do back home, on the farm where she grew up.

"It was fun until it wasn't," she explained, gregarious and with a voice louder than you'd normally hear in a library. "My daddy wanted a boy, so I was raised to do anything a son might and learned to do it better than most."

"Why'd you leave?" Arden asked, while Ronan was checking

out the freshly arrived new releases. *They must have come on the same boat as me,* Arden thought. She hadn't realized it at the time.

"I got to feeling for the cattle, you know," Rhonda said, pulling at the sleeve of her faded denim shirt. "Couldn't deal with it all after a while, wouldn't even eat meat. Got into it with my dad, started spending more time away from home. Met some interesting people, read some interesting books. Got me some new ideas on how to be."

"Your father wasn't pleased?" Arden guessed.

Rhonda let out a booming laugh. "Wasn't pleased? Girl, my father threw me out. But it turned out to be a blessing in disguise if I ever saw one. Three years later, the farm burned down in a wildfire that got out of control. My brothers scattered in the wind. Daddy drank himself to death."

"I'm sorry."

"That's life." Rhonda shrugged. "I got out, though," she went on. "Moved in with some friends in the city, got a job, started taking college classes at night. See, I used to think my world was as big as the Montana sky, but I was wrong. Back in Montana, only the sky was big. It took me leaving to see it right. Afterward, I sought the world as long as I wanted."

Arden smiled, encouragingly. "And?"

"And I got it, for a while. Traveled and everything. And then I realized maybe it wasn't the size, but the quality." Rhonda grinned happily. "So I started looking around and found Ronan."

At the sound of his name, Ronan looked up from the books. "That you did," he said.

"As easy as that?" Arden pushed.

"Oh, no." Rhonda waved a large hand. "Nothing easy about it. More aptitude tests and interviews than any college application process. Or any job, for that matter. One hoop after the next." She laughed good-naturedly, and Ronan did a mock guilty shrug and smiled to play along.

"But you jumped through every single one?" Arden asked.

"You bet I did," Rhonda replied proudly. "If I set my mind on something, I'm as stubborn as any bull I've ever met, and I've met quite a few."

"And you've chosen library work?"

"As opposed to farming, you mean?"

"I'm just asking," Arden said, holding up her hands, wondering if she had offended the woman.

"Nah, I'm just messing with you." Rhonda laughed. "I love books, so yeah, here I am. Am I above doing a bit of farming and livestock consulting on the side? Heck no. But being among books is my happy place."

"I get that," Arden said. "It's a lovely library. Is it just you here?"

"Janice, too. Have you met Janice?"

Arden shook her head.

"You will. She's great. Our local archivist, among other things. Used to be a proper rocket scientist, if you can believe it. She's here most days. Not today, though, so far."

"I'm sure she'll be in later," Ronan interjected. "She just had to take a look at something this morning."

Something that makes a noise like a sonic boom, Arden thought. No point alarming or antagonizing anyone.

She was surprised when Rhonda didn't question it, though. Was everyone here just *that* calm? She had a neighbor like that once. A perpetual stoner, never even mildly perturbed. Slept through fire alarms.

Not that these people were stoned, despite the obvious presence of cannabis on the island. Their calm had a different timbre to it. Something like profound contentment.

"Love the unicorns," Arden told the woman, pivoting. "Out front. What a great idea."

"Franklin and Avram, in case you were wondering."

"As in Ben Franklin, I'm guessing. And Avram?"

Rhonda put her hand over her heart in mock offense. "Henriette Avram. Only one of the most significant contributors to digital cataloging of our time and the developer of MARC format."

"Marc?"

"MARC. Machine-Readable Cataloging. She came up with it in the late sixties and early seventies and implemented it at the Library of Congress. It made possible the automation of many library functions, enabling electronic sharing of bibliographic information between libraries using preexisting cataloging standards. Shame not more people know about her."

"I had no idea," Arden admitted. "But I do now. Thank you."

"Well, that's why people come to the library, isn't it?" Rhonda smiled. "To learn something new."

"See?" Ronan said. "This is why Rhonda belongs here with us."

Arden nodded but couldn't help mentally picking at his words. What did it mean? Was Rhonda just the right kind of nerdy? A correct sort of enthusiast? What was Ronan prescreening these people for? Intelligence? Passion? What if it was darker than that? What if they were predominantly single, rejected by society, unlikely to be missed?

Ronan was promoting the message of hope and change, but would it sell an article? Because a scandal would. Unquestionably so. Cynical perspective, sure, but scandal was the axis the world turned on. Arden couldn't help but look for it, even though all these perfectly happy people with their perfectly content lives appeared hellbent on obstructing her quest.

After the thank yous and nice to meet yous, they reemerged into the street, under the now-relentless sun.

"So what is it?" she asked Ronan directly, wondering if that was the right approach. "How do you choose? How did you choose Rhonda?"

"We have complex predictive algorithms on top of a variety of personality and aptitude tests," he began. It sounded rehearsed, or at least as if it had been said dozens of times before.

"Come on." She met his eyes. "The real answer."

His lips stretched into a sly smile. "Imagine yourself on a small island with an enormous task before you. Would you want Rhonda on your team?"

Arden thought of the woman. Her strong hands, her quick smile, her easygoing, can-do personality. "Sure," she said.

"Well, there you go." Ronan grinned. "It doesn't have to be more complicated than that. Now, where to next?"

CHAPTER 7.
JACOB.

THE TRIP FELT shorter the second time around. The dog was weaving in between their feet while Janice entertained them with true stories of objects falling from the sky.

"The Chicxulub Event. Sixty-five million years ago. Estimated damage, seventy percent of life on Earth. Tunguska Event. June 30th, 1908. Estimated force, twelve megatons. Estimated damage, eighty million trees." She spat these tidbits out like baseball stats. Dispassionate, matter-of-factly. But all Jacob could think about were those numbers. All that terrible devastation. "The Chelyabinsk Event. 2013. Exploded in the air, limiting effect. Shockwave created. Estimated damage, seventy-two hundred buildings across six cities, and fifteen hundred people injured, mostly by broken glass."

"Woof," Terry exclaimed. "That's awful."

"Woof," Jupi echoed, pleased someone finally spoke his language.

"But," Jacob started tentatively, "those objects were huge, weren't they?"

"Sure," Janice said. "Twenty and thirty meters in diameter on the last two, much larger on the first one."

"This one is small," Jacob pointed out.

"If it's even a space ball," Terry put in. "Could be something else, in theory."

"Exactly," Janice agreed. "Best not to jump to any conclusions until we have a chance to examine it."

They came upon the clearing soon enough. Jacob was surprised to see that the object was still glowing, albeit faintly. He had hoped it would have stopped by now, turning it into something innocuous looking, like a smaller bowling ball. The glowing created an undeniably malevolent effect.

"Would you look at that?" Janice said, her voice quiet and full of what Jacob thought was awe.

They were all staring in the same direction but seeing vastly different things.

The smell was still there, but it had changed into something distinctly . . . meatier? Bloodier?

The dog had picked up on it right away, his olfactory powers so much more fine-tuned than his bipedal companions. Pawing at his snout, he whimpered and backed away.

"Oh come on, buddy." Janice extended her hand to him. "Don't be like that."

Jupi continued his retreat. His owner smiled at him indulgently, then proceeded to approach the object in the clearing.

"Should you be, um, getting so close to it?" Jacob asked.

Janice didn't stop.

"What about space radiation?" Jacob said louder, dragging out his limited knowledge based on an old Neil deGrasse Tyson book he once read. Or maybe it was something he saw on PBS's *Nova*.

He wasn't sure if that was the sort of thing that lingered or got stripped away on the journey down, but the object glowed. It freaking *glowed*. That had to count for something.

"The way I figure, this space ball of yours has more to fear from us than we from it," Janice said, voice loud enough to carry without turning around. "I brought gloves with me, just in case, to handle it."

Jacob turned to Terry and raised his eyebrows as if to say, "Should we do something?"

The big man shifted from foot to foot and shrugged. He looked uncomfortable with the entire thing, like he wished he was miles away, preferably in his bed or his bakery—the two places he proclaimed to love most in this world.

Reluctantly, Jacob started after Janice, pulling up his sweatshirt over his face against the smell. For a moment, he thought the ground vibrated against the soles of his shoes the closer he went, but that couldn't have been right. Unless they were experiencing a small seismic event. Was such a thing even possible here? Could the ground be experiencing some sort of aftershock?

He focused on Janice's back, but she cut a small and narrow figure, doing hardly anything to obscure the main attraction before them. He tried looking at the earth under his feet, but it was impossible to keep his eyes down. The object ahead commanded his attention.

Janice stopped a few feet away. Jacob followed suit.

"Would you look at that," she said with some degree of reverence. "All this time of quiet, and this thing booms into our lives."

"I wouldn't mind it if it boomed right back out of them," Jacob mumbled.

She gave him a disapproving look.

"What?"

"This, my friend, is a bona fide miracle. A gift from the universe. And though you're young, I know you're smart enough to appreciate it," Janice said sternly, reminding him of an old high school teacher.

In any other circumstance, Jacob would likely disagree with her on both the former and the latter estimation, no matter how flattering they may be. He was, after all, practically middle aged now, not that much younger than Janice herself, and as for smart— he didn't really feel it. Too many mistakes, too many wasted years. The only truly smart thing he'd ever done was come to the island.

Maybe Janice was right. Maybe this *was* something special that his negative thinking doomed based on the sheer unwelcome surprise and panic-laden fear that inevitably came with it.

"Should we—" he started, but Janice hushed him. While he mused, she had taken out an electronic gadget that looked like something out of a science fiction movie and proceeded to scan the area.

"Perhaps we should err on the side of caution," she said, frowning at the digital readout. "Just to be safe." She produced a foil blanket out of her backpack, one of those things victims in TV shows always got wrapped in upon being rescued, and threw it over the object.

"Is that going to be enough?" Jacob asked.

"Should be," she replied, and he wondered if the island's general relaxed demeanor had gotten to Janice too. His own gut had been churning with anxiety so violently he could barely stand upright. The closer he got to this thing, the more it threw off his equilibrium.

BEAUTIFUL, ONCE

By now the oceanic swooshing in his ears was nearly as loud as Janice's voice. He tried breathing and focusing, but the sound dropped in and out. When it cleared, he noticed just how quiet it was out here. No birds singing, no wind rustling the trees. Nothing.

Nature, it seemed, abhorred its intruder as much as Jacob did.

"Heavy bastard, isn't he?" Janice said. He hadn't even realized she'd been trying to shift the thing out of the ground. "Give me a hand, Jacob, will you?"

He would have preferred to cut off his hand and throw it into the ocean, but there was no polite way to refuse.

Long ago, he'd learned that it didn't matter how his gut and his mind churned on the inside, so long as he put on a good show on the outside. What people saw—what we let people see of ourselves—was all that really mattered. And here on the island, where cooperation was everything, he couldn't just say no.

Slowly, he bent his protesting knees and reached out his shaking arms to help.

It was no good. Small as the object was, and now slippery in its shiny blanket, it weighed as much as a ton of bricks. How could that be?

Up close, the smell, barely ameliorated by the foil-like fabric, felt like a punch to the face. Jacob gagged, excused himself, and gagged again.

"You okay?" Janice asked, shooting him a concerned look. "Don't you go hurling on the thing. It would make a terrible first impression."

He knew she was joking but couldn't bring himself to laugh. Even words were an effort.

"Terry," he finally pushed out. "Terry could probably move it." They both turned around to shout at the big man to come.

Terry looked the way Jacob felt, like he wanted to decline and didn't know how. Slowly, he started walking toward them.

Jacob gagged again. "Sorry."

"What's with you?" she asked gently. "You okay?"

"You don't smell it?" he replied incredulously with a question of his own.

"There's a bit of odor, I suppose," she said slowly. "But it isn't terrible or anything. Makes me think of petrichor and barbecues."

What the hell is petrichor? Jacob wondered. He was about to ask when he felt Terry's heavy hand land on his shoulder.

"What's up?"

"Can't lift it," Jacob replied, taking care to speak louder.

Terry grinned and made a show of flexing his muscles. "Must be a job for Superman," he quipped, lowering himself to get a better angle.

He heaved the object up but miscalculated. The weight threw off his balance, landing him on his butt in what would have been a comical fashion under any other circumstances. Or maybe it was objectively funny to anyone but Jacob, since Janice guffawed, and Terry joined her.

"What's this thing made of?" he asked her. "Lead?"

"Lead's nothing." She waved the thought off. "Do you know that a cubic centimeter of neutronium weighs roughly four hundred million tons?"

"Say that again?" Terry gestured to his ears, prompting her to speak up.

Janice repeated her words louder.

"Damn. Thought maybe I heard you wrong the first time. What is neutronium exactly?"

"It's what neutron stars are made of."

"Tell us more."

Janice smiled like a teacher asked to explain her favorite subject. "Think of a giant star, something eight to twenty times larger than the sun. When it dies, it explodes, goes supernova. But its core, still huge at this point, remains intact. Then, it too begins to collapse on itself, getting denser and denser. Long story short, it shrinks dramatically while retaining the same mass, which is how it ends up being the heaviest known object in the universe."

"And that's what we got here?" Terry asked, scratching his head.

"I don't think so." Janice laughed. "An African elephant on average weighs about four tons. So a cubic centimeter of neutronium would be the equivalent of a hundred million elephants. And this thing is considerably larger than a cubic centimeter, and we have already shifted it a bit."

Terry made a comic mind explosion gesture.

"We just gotta put our backs into it," Janice assured them.

Sure enough, Terry got at the object from a new angle, rocking it side to side. Turned out, the biggest thing was dislodging it from the ground. Afterward, it was something Terry claimed he could easily carry by himself and made good on it, though Jacob thought he saw the strain in the big man's face.

Jupi ran either to the side or ahead of them, never getting too close, and Jacob couldn't help but think the dog was the only sensible one out of all of them.

"Should have brought a wheelbarrow," Janice said. But it didn't matter. Eventually, Terry got the object to her house. Or rather, the shed out back which she referred to as her lab.

The place was s small rectangle with a large table and shelves covering every wall. Jacob wasn't sure he could name all the things crammed in there. But Janice moved among it all like some modern day Victor Frankenstein, a person of science perfectly in her element.

Terry left the object in the middle of the table, where Janice had cleared a space for it.

"Thank you, gentlemen," she said. "May I get you some lemonade for your trouble?"

Terry gratefully accepted, and they followed her into the main house that was, unlike the lab, perfectly neat. Infinitely more relaxing, books replaced the vials littering the lab. Though, Jacob still didn't think he could drink a sip. His insides felt too tightly interwoven by anxiety.

Jupi hung back outside, softly growling at the lab shed. "You're being so weird," Janice told him, shaking her head.

He did a passable impression of a cocked eyebrow back as if to say, "I'm not the weird one here."

Terry chugged a tall glass of homemade lemonade while Jacob busied himself perusing the book titles on one of the shelves.

"Want to borrow something?" Janice asked.

"Nah, I'm still on that Alderman novel for the book club," he replied. Lately, he seemed to doze off about ten pages in with a peculiar and frustrating regularity. It wasn't the book's fault, by any means; his eyes just kept closing.

"That's a good one," Janice said, brushing her hand through her short hair. "Going to be a fun discussion, I'm sure."

He forced himself to smile politely.

His skin was itching the way it tended to when he ate too much chocolate, though he always insisted it wasn't an allergy. Perhaps it was merely his internal discomfort manifesting externally. He imagined sinking his fingernails into his skin, drawing them up and down, creating bloody furrows until the itch went away. It was only in his arms. The last thing he touched with them was the glowing object. Did it do something to him?

Jacob bit the inside of his bottom lip, forcing himself to focus on his immediate surroundings. If he wasn't careful, he knew he was likely to spiral right into a full-blown panic attack. He already felt the shortness of breath encroaching. At least, he *could* breathe. No more of that infernal stench.

Janice and Terry were talking about space. The sound drifted in and out of Jacob's ears, past the rushing swoosh of his blood. Where Janice was science, Terry was mostly pure speculation. He knew enough of the sensationalized headlines, but not the technical details behind it all. And he remained strongly curious about the space poop.

"We should go," Jacob said. "Update Martha, so she can tell Ronan. Keep everyone in the loop. I bet Ronan's dying to know."

"I bet he's busy with that pretty journalist lady," Terry joked.

Jacob shrugged. He'd heard of the new arrival but had yet to lay eyes on her. Either way, he wasn't sure about the entire thing. Ronan wanted to put the word out there, spread the message. Sure, Jacob got that. But inviting a journalist into their mix seemed like the wrong way to go about it.

Besides, no matter how pretty she was, he doubted Ronan cared. The man with his looks, money, and charm could have anyone yet he seemed perfectly content alone. Less of a reclusive eccentric, more of a man who'd tried it all and got tired of it.

Jacob had thought about it often and never quite understood it. He felt that in Ronan's shoes, he would have charted an entirely different course for himself. For one thing, he couldn't imagine someone like Ronan Bard ever struggling with the same issues as he had. In what world did that man ever not fit in?

Except he was here with the rest of them, so what did Jacob know?

They had spoken before, on a number of occasions, from the initial interview on, but Jacob had never really gotten the sense of him. Ronan was the sort of man one might wish to be without knowing exactly how to go about it.

He said interesting, intelligent things. And sometimes he said strange, wildly controversial ones. But it was difficult to know to what extent he meant them, or if some of it was merely a performance. The one thing Jacob had unshakable confidence in was Ronan's belief in this place they were all a part of. That was enough.

He caught himself scratching his arm and forcibly stopped, balling his hands and shoving them in his pockets.

"Come on, Terry. Let's go."

The big man thanked Janice for the lemonade, while she thanked him for his labor, but eventually, the pleasantries were over, and they were outside. Jupi eyed them from a nearby tree but didn't come to say bye the way he always did. A suspect behavior, Jacob thought, for one of the friendliest members of the island community.

"You think she's home?" Terry asked.

"Martha? Nah. Probably at Ronan's."

They began walking in that direction. Jacob concentrated on every step, every breath, every word. Anything to keep calm.

"We should stop by the lumberjacks, too. Let them know about the trees."

"Right," Jacob said.

BEAUTIFUL, ONCE

By some amusing happenstance, the woodsmen crew consisted of several men named Jack. Technically one of them was Jackson and one was John, but they all went by Jack prior to coming here, and ever since.

Jackson used to own a gym. John wrestled professionally until he received one too many concussions. Jacob wasn't sure what the others had done before. Some people wanted to talk about it, some preferred to leave the past in the past. He belonged to the latter category, much like the majority of others.

"What's with you, man? Are you okay?"

Jacob glanced up. Terry looked concerned, his eyebrows furrowing into a low V.

"What do you mean?"

"I don't know." Terry shook his head and adjusted his hat. "You've just seemed off ever since we found the thing. And you didn't even have to lug it all the way out here."

"Yeah, I'm fine," Jacob lied. He rubbed his forehead. "I just . . . I mean, it's weird, isn't it? That thing? The way it glows? The smell?"

Agree with me, he thought, *Tell me I'm not losing my mind. I've gotten so used to my newfound sanity here on the island, and I don't want to jeopardize it.*

"I guess it's kind of weird." Terry shrugged. "But kind of exciting, too, no? Something different from kneading dough all day, right?"

Jacob chortled. "Thought you liked kneading dough."

"Sure I do," Terry said. "Beats construction work."

"But?"

"But nothing. It's dough balls every day of the week, but today it's space balls, you know? Pretty freaking awesome, don't you think?"

Jacob shrugged. His right hand found his left arm and began scratching. He forced himself to stop by sinking his fingernails into the irritated flesh, the way his grandfather once taught him to do with particularly itchy bites.

"You worry too much," Terry said, slapping him on the back. "Seriously, you do. Ever think of getting something to help you mellow out? I hear Tru's new blend is the bomb."

"Trust me, that's the last thing I need." Jacob found himself getting annoyed at the conversation. Objective awareness of the fact that Terry was his friend who meant well did nothing to the very subjective desire to yell at him and tell him to shut up.

Jacob, who'd never been much of a yeller—more of a sulker—didn't understand the impulse and did his best to push it down.

He was glad when Ronan's house came into view. Finally, something actionable. The man wasn't home, though. Neither was Martha.

They stopped by one of the Jack's houses next. The door was open. The invitation to come in was a shout from the living room.

Jack was sitting on a well-worn couch along with the other Jack, playing video games on a console that had to be ancient by now.

"Who's winning?" Terry asked.

"I am." The blond Jack grinned.

"Like hell you are," said his friend. Jack McCollough had shaggy reddish hair and beard, resembling a highland bull in both appearance and temperament.

"What's up, fellas?"

"Got a job for you," Terry said, his eyes following the frantic fight scene on screen.

"You don't say?" The blond Jack hit the pause button.

"Saved by the bell," his friend harrumphed. "I was just about to knock you out."

"Doubt it. What's the job?"

Terry explained while Jacob stood there, chewing his lip, feeling his fingernails dig crescent moons into his palms.

"Neat," the blond Jack summed up after Terry finished.

"Yeah, we'll get right on it after I finish kicking his butt," Jack McCollough said, emphatically jabbing at the controller buttons.

Terry and Jacob let themselves out.

"I wonder if I should have gone into that business," Terry said as they walked away. "The bakery is making me soft," he added, patting his ample gut.

"Not too late," Jacob joked. "You'll be the only lumber-Terry,"

"Who's going to bake then?"

"Someone else. Someone new. Maybe we'll get some fresh blood coming in after whatever this journalist writes."

"You think?"

"Why not?"

Terry nodded his head to the idea. "Yeah, that could be good." They walked in silence for a beat. "You ever miss it?" Terry asked. "The mainland. Your old life. All the people. I mean, not that I'm complaining. Everyone here is great, but it's the same faces day in and day out, you know."

Jacob flashed back to his life before the island: the endless procession of disappointing interactions and anxiety, like the kind that had been riding him since morning but on a daily basis—the constant exhausting effort of trying and failing to fit in, the endless balancing of uppers and downers just to get from sunrise to sunset.

"No, I don't miss it at all," he said honestly.

Terry nodded. "That's the spirit," he boomed, pounding a large fist in the air.

Anything else would have had the conversation sliding dangerously toward complaining, a thing unofficially frowned upon. It wasn't any kind of rule, simply something that came out of one of Ronan's speeches.

"People complain too much," he had said. It wasn't a Ted Talk but something similar, possibly something on PBS. Jacob couldn't remember.

"They spend more time talking about what's wrong than trying to change it. Mind you, there is nothing inherently wrong with complaining so long as it helps you establish the problem. But if it continues, endlessly and fruitlessly, well then . . ." Ronan had slapped his hands together, a startlingly loud sound. "That's a problem in and of itself."

He smiled, confidence personified.

"I think talk is cheap only when it doesn't lead to action. I believe in proactive solutions. I'm a big fan of change, carving your own path, building your own destiny. I've spoken to people who told me to my face, 'Well, sure, easy for you to say, you can *buy* your own destiny.' And I had to remind them that I was born with nothing. Same as most. Nothing but potential. I earned everything I have now. I earned the right and the privilege to be here talking to you."

He had pushed his blond hair back from his forehead, never breaking eye contact. Jacob had always been amazed by how clearly he remembered those appearances, those interviews, replaying them in his mind like scenes from his favorite movie.

"I would not presume to tell you how to live your life," Ronan Bard had said; it felt like he had spoken directly to him. "But here you are, listening to me. So maybe you are curious. Maybe you want something more for yourself, something better. Well, I can promise you one thing: you will not get there by complaining." He grinned. "Get off your ass and do something."

Jacob had always made fun of motivational speakers and the entire self-help genre wagon they rode in on. He wasn't sure why or how he let Ronan Bard get straight into his psyche, but he did. The man's words, his message, had resonated with Jacob deeply. He wanted more; he thought bigger.

And the thing with that was once you started, you couldn't stop. If you allowed for the possibility of a larger world, your own began to feel like a trap. If you allowed for the possibility of a better life, your own began to hold no appeal. And Ronan's island, which both conceptually and geographically seemed a million miles away, began to feel like the next step. Like the future.

The place was small enough that one thorough loop would likely have you come across anyone you might be looking for. They found Martha enjoying a glass of orange juice on a bench outside the café as was her custom most mornings. There was a pair of orange trees directly behind the café in a small sitting area, so the freshness was unparalleled. As Ingrid, one of the owners and a big fan of puns, put it: "Palpable and pulpable."

Martha straightened out her back upon seeing them, assuming a more businesslike posture.

"Well, gentlemen?"

"The object is in Janice's lab and the lumberjack team is on its way to take care of the trees," Jacob reported.

"Excellent." Martha pressed her lips into a tight smile. "Thank you so much. Don't let me keep you from your day further."

They left, feeling dismissed, but also glad of it.

"Is that Ronan and the reporter woman?" Terry asked, squinting at the distance.

Jacob followed his eye line and confirmed. "You should really get some glasses."

"Don't like the way they look on me."

"Contacts?"

"No way am I touching my eyeballs."

Jacob sighed. "Just wait till you start getting the baking ingredients mixed up."

"Ha." The big man took off his hat, ran his hand over his shaved head, and put it back on. He had long ago taken off his fleece and tied it around his waist, and was now profusely sweating through his T-shirt. "That's never going to happen. Everything I need to do in that kitchen I can do with my eyes closed by now."

His mother was a big baker, Terry had told Jacob some time ago when they were still getting to know each other. He grew up helping her in the kitchen but only when his father wasn't around. Cauley Sr. was a man's man, approving only of testosterone-laden traditional pursuits like hunting, drinking, building. He was the louder, stronger, pushier of the parents, and Terry felt like he had no choice but to follow him into the construction business. The old man ended up breaking his back after falling on a roofing gig. That took care of hunting and building, and only left drinking. Terry stuck by the job. All it cost him was his hearing but not before he heard the siren call of a better life.

Here on the island, he happily reignited the old passion, glad for the chance to reinvent himself. His pies were second to none and his sourdough starter was in high demand year after year. It was likely that the man could indeed do it all blindfolded by now, but middle age had found his eyes too tired and blurring anything at a distance.

"You'll never survive the apocalypse this way," Jacob joked. "You won't know what's coming."

"Maybe," Terry agreed, playing along. "But I'd be able to take care of any threat within reach better than most."

That much was true, too. Jacob didn't favor his own apocalypse survival chances too highly.

"Is she a looker or what?" Terry asked.

Jacob took in the woman's lithe form, dressed plainly but stylishly, with shoulder-length, tousled dark hair, pale skin, and almond-shaped eyes. He was bad with ages, but if he had to guess, early thirties.

"Yeah," he said simply.

Terry grinned. "Should we go over there, introduce ourselves?"

"It's a small place, I'm sure our turn will come organically."

The big man shook his head. "Jacob Gurley. I don't know if there's blood in those veins of yours or motor oil."

"Speaking of which, I really got to get to work," Jacob said. The morning had discombobulated him enough to almost forget about it. Now it all rushed back in, a welcome wave of responsibilities and chores to distract him from negative thoughts and that horrible itching,

"Sure." Terry squinted at the distance again. "Where does it look like they're headed?"

"The farm, I think."

"Yeah, that makes sense." Terry mopped his forehead with the back of his palm. "Not to worry, though. Sooner or later everyone needs something freshly baked."

"That's right. I may stop by for lunch. But until then . . ." Jacob smacked his friend playfully on his massive bicep and took off.

Tony was already there when he got to the shop, his skin

glistening with sweat as he worked. "Late morning, boss?" he quipped.

They didn't have anything like a boss and employee structure. Never did. Depending on the amount of work needed to be done, Mox occasionally came by to help out. Of the three of them, she was the only one who'd been a grease monkey back on the mainland, too. Her preference was for fixing up the larger equipment, and they both suspected she secretly missed cars.

Jacob and Tony were mostly enthusiastic amateurs who picked up the trade as they went along, supplementing knowledge acquired over the years with things learned from books or on the go. Whatever it took to keep the island machinery chugging along.

"Heard that boom this morning?" Tony asked, while Jacob pushed up his sleeves, looking over the to-do list for the day.

"Yep. In fact, that's why I'm late." Just being in the shop, among the familiar smells and sounds, soothed Jacob's mind. If only it had worked on his skin. "Terry and I went to check it out."

"And?"

"And it might be some sort of space debris. Janice is on the case now, so she'll figure it out."

"Oh yeah, she will." Like Janice, Tony grew up wanting to be an astronaut. He never got as close to NASA as Janice did and quietly worshipped the woman for it.

He went back to rewiring an old-fashioned record player.

"How's it coming along?" Jacob asked, reaching to pick up some fallen screws and put them back on the table.

"It's co—Dude, what's with your arm?"

Jacob looked. The underside of his forearm had some kind of rash on it. Difficult to tell if it was caused by his scratching or the cause of his scratching. An unsightly thing either way. He pulled the arm away, pushing his sleeve down over it. He didn't even notice it before, too absorbed by the list of things to do.

"Probably got into some poison ivy out in the woods," he mumbled.

"Is there poison ivy there?"

"Sure. It's everywhere," Jacob replied, uncertain if that was right.

The rash was red and angry looking, and just seeing it made him want to scratch and scratch. He shook his head. It looked too much like an outward sign of his internal turmoil. Too close for comfort. It wouldn't do. He'd get some aloe to put on it, and that would be that.

Jacob turned to the bicycle with a damaged front wheel. It would need truing and a new tire. He rubbed his now sleeve-covered arm against his side. It was better than scratching. Then he set about taking off the wheel, humming to himself.

When Tony asked him what the tune was, he couldn't name it.

"It's the tune that record player of yours *should* be playing," he said, immediately regretting it, feeling like a jerk.

Tony frowned but shrugged it off. "Give me till the end of the day, and this baby will purr," he said.

Jacob checked himself, biting his lip against any other stupid comments. He worked on the wheel slowly, steadily, replacing the damaged spokes. When the itch got unbearable, he stuck one of the spokes under his sleeve to drag it across the irritated skin. It was what he did as a kid, when he had a cast on his leg after he played Superman and learned about gravity the hard way.

He thought he felt the metal penetrating his skin and bit his lips harder to keep himself from crying out. The sheer momentary relief though was enough to make him swoon with pleasure. He closed his eyes, letting the wheel spin and spin.

CHAPTER 8.
MARTHA.

S HE SAW RONAN and Arden walking toward the farm and thought, *Of course. How can you have a tour of a sustainable, self-contained community without a trip to the farm?*

Martha didn't grow up around animals, although later in life her mother acquired one of those bizarre hairless cats to dote on. Pets remained by and large a foreign concept to her, used as a poor substitute for a partner or children. Martha knew that statistically speaking she had the makings of a cat lady and vowed to never become one. And dogs: Dogs were simply too much work. In all her life, she had only found one being worthy of such attention, and fortunately Ronan groomed and took care of himself.

Martha knew they'd have to have a farm on the island, just as they'd need a functional agricultural system, but was glad to leave it to someone else. She could manage logistics and financials but had no interest in the livestock itself.

Over the years, living so close to it had changed her. Though she hadn't meant to, she began to think differently about what she ate and where her food came from. They didn't keep cattle because of methane, but there were goats, and sheep, and chickens. You couldn't help but be aware of where your milk, eggs, and sweaters came from. More often than not, it made her turn to seafood, which to her looked as close to inanimate as a live creature could and therefore palatable enough to eat.

There were many vegetarians and vegans on the island, cultivating soybeans and such for their protein. She appreciated that, but it seemed like too much work. Martha preferred to reserve her brain space for things other than food.

Ronan, on the other hand, loved animals. He found them more worthy of love than most people, he used to joke, but as with most of his jokes, there was a lot of truth there. He was probably telling Arden that right now, seeing if it made her smile.

Throughout their time together, Martha had learned most of his narrative gimmicks and patois, the easy way with which he charmed the newcomers. He loved meeting new people, but the feeling was tough to sustain. As a child, Martha mused, he likely loved new toys at first, then set them aside once he figured out their tricks.

Martha had sensed that about him early on, his restlessness, and vowed to herself to never become a brick in that wall for him. And because she knew she wasn't exciting enough to hold Ronan's attention indefinitely, she made herself indispensable instead. Someone he could not afford to get tired of.

Arden was his shiny new toy now, and that was fine. The man had that kind of maddening energy, an insatiable appetite for life. It needed fuel.

Martha had always been a bit surprised deep down that Ronan stayed put on the island for so long. She used to think he'd eventually get done with it all and leave. It would be a graceful exit of a beloved patriarch, one where he'd promise to check in frequently and visit often. He'd go on, have some more adventures, do some more exploring, then come back for a while. It would be a cycle, a rhythm of their lives, like the rising and setting of the sun. But no: Whatever or whoever had broken his heart before they met, appeared to have done a pretty thorough job, leaving only a sparkle where a flame once burned brightly.

She still saw it in Ronan on occasion, after all this time. She recognized a disappointment with life all too well, having seen it in the mirror for years and years in her own eyes.

And so he stayed. And she stayed. And time went on and on, until you looked back and could not believe how much time had passed.

Ronan had his passions—ones he liked to refer to as his hobbies. She wondered if he would tell Arden about them. Not many people knew, after all. He kept a part of himself separate and had his very own fortress of solitude at the far end of the island to accommodate it. The islanders, in a collective display of respectful privacy, didn't go there.

Martha had seen it, of course, but she'd always been far too concerned with terrestrial matters to stargaze. The equipment was devastatingly expensive, but Ronan could afford it. That was primarily all she cared about as far as that place went.

She thought she ought to stop by Janice's and see about the object. The woman fascinated her. In another life, she thought they might have been friends. A real friendship, not the good-natured, proximity-based neighborliness they shared now. Janice was fiercely smart, determined, and embittered by how little any of that got her back on the mainland. Martha recognized herself in the woman. The similarities ended there; Janice had a heart where Martha was all brain.

Janice was married before. Martha knew as much because she'd read everyone's file, but that was only good for broad strokes. The files contained salient facts without details to make them real. She knew the people on the island as a collection of statistics first, a skeletal structure at best. Only later, through personal interaction, did she add meat to those bones, as it were, to flesh out each individual.

And now Janice had Jupi, her second dog—one she was dearly devoted to. The first one was a similar-looking mutt, albeit with more golden retriever to him. Janice had brought him here with her when she moved, and he died of old age a few years later. Martha could not remember his name.

Jupiter came along a few months later as a puppy from the litter of the dog owned by the taciturn ferryman. Ronan had gotten him as a birthday gift for Janice. He was always good at thoughtful gestures.

Martha liked Jupi more than any dog she'd ever met, but still couldn't imagine living with or taking care of him. There were some pets on the island, and a bit of local wildlife, all of which had left her fairly indifferent. So long as nothing crept and crawled near her, she was content.

When Ronan was looking around for islands—there was a rather robust market, Martha was surprised to learn—she had pleaded for somewhere without snakes. Or giant spiders.

"Okay, okay." He laughed. "I guess I won't buy Australia."

"Well, you shouldn't anyway," she tried to joke back. "It would be a terrible investment. So much of that land is unlivable."

He seemed to appreciate the effort. "Don't worry," he told her. "I'll find us a paradise on Earth."

And he did, of course. When she allowed herself, during rare moments free of practical thought, she enjoyed it here. It felt like home.

Then the worrying brain turned back on, and she questioned if all of this would last. What if their fearless leader got restless? Her mind kept returning to that.

She used to worry that middle age might do it, but Ronan's Dorian Gray-like approach to getting older betrayed nothing—except here was Arden, young and slick, like the human equivalent of a sports car. Arden to charm, Arden to impress. And here was Ronan, showing off, preening ever so subtly.

Martha shook her head. Her brain was going into overdrive. She knew just the thing for it. A practical solution to an impractical problem. Never complain about what can be fixed. One of Ronan's mottos, unsurprisingly effective. She course corrected to the bakery.

One of the best things about never being skinny was never worrying about it. She used to before, on the mainland, where such things inevitably mattered, but never here. She'd never been much of a foodie, but on the island, she usually ate what she wanted, within reason, and what she wanted now was a pastry.

There was a strong sense of utilitarianism in the first buildings on the island. Ronan didn't care for it. He said the architecture should be fun. "The place should look like fun," he explained emphatically. "Like somewhere your inner child would be happy to play, and your adult self would be happy to live."

They shuffled through several architects until they stumbled upon Neils Dahl at last. Tall, slim, and linen-blond with a crisp Scandinavian edge to his vowels, the man understood Ronan's vision, transforming the island's buildings into purpose-built structures.

Subsequently, the bakery looked precisely like a bakery in one's imagination; it was shaped like a muffin. Or, some insisted, a cupcake.

Dahl had even planned out the overall layout of the main street with its small park. His original vision was that of a center hub with streets and buildings radiating from it, much like a bike wheel. The man was a devoted cyclist.

Ronan enjoyed Dahl's company immensely and was sad to see him leave, though he hid it well.

"I invited him to stay over and over," he told Martha, shaking his head. She'd never been good at comforting, but over the years she had perfected a sort of calm listening that could pass as offered solace.

"He said this world was lovely but much too small." Ronan rubbed his chin. "I feel like I was set up for a crude *size doesn't matter* joke." He smiled but there was sadness in it.

Martha waited patiently, wondering if perhaps there was more to Ronan's feelings for Dahl, but never asked. It was a strange thing to know someone well enough to read them like an open book in so many respects yet have them be a complete mystery in others.

She knew the minute details of his days but not who broke his heart so thoroughly back on the mainland. And here on the island where secrets were virtually impossible to hide, he'd never had any romantic entanglements. She had her suspicions about the clandestine trips to the mainland, perhaps during the times he secluded himself in his place on the other side of the island. It wouldn't be too difficult to keep or charter a boat for those times, to come and go unseen. But she granted him his privacy and kept her questions to herself.

She respected him and his judgment. It was as simple as that. Love was a complicated thing, but respect was easy.

Martha entered the oversized muffin of a shop, which never failed to make her feel a bit like Alice.

"Terry," she greeted the large man behind the counter, taking care to speak up.

"Martha," he replied.

She perused the displays out of habit, though she seldom varied her order. Something looked a bit off. She tried to put a finger on it, but she realized that perhaps it was the baker himself. It wasn't unusual for a large man to get sweaty working around hot ovens, but Terry looked drenched. His hat barely managed to keep the sweat from running into his eyes, and his shirt was plastered to his body under the colorful, flour-stained apron.

Martha wasn't sure what to say or how to say it. "Thanks again for taking care of that space ball," she said instead.

"Oh, sure." Terry waved his giant mitt. "How often do you find something like that? Here or anywhere." He blinked away some of the sweat.

"I was thinking of stopping by Janice's in a while, seeing what she thinks," Martha told him. She studied the baked goods on display, finally realizing what was off about them—the shapes.

Terry was usually very precise, engineer-like in his creations. It was as if he brought his construction background to his baking, ensuring his product was neat enough to stack if need be, just like bricks in the wall. Perfectly shaped loaves, neatly rounded donuts, precise cookie circles.

Today things looked like Dali's melting clocks, though not as extreme. Everything appeared to be liquefying, along with its creator.

"Is everything okay, Terry?" Martha blurted out uncharacteristically.

"Yeah, great." He smiled, wiping his forehead with the back of his hand, seemingly clueless as to what was going on. "The usual for you?"

The last thing Martha wanted right now was a bran muffin. In fact, she seemed to have lost her appetite altogether.

"Hot in here, isn't it?" she said carefully.

"Same as always. Slightly north of Hell," he joked.

"Don't know how you can stand it," she sympathized. It had to be like getting caught in a perpetual hot flash, she figured. A hellish proposition.

He grinned. The sweat ran in rivulets along his laugh lines. "Mind over matter," he said. "Though having spent so much of my life working construction outside in all weather, I'm not complaining."

No, of course not, she thought. It wouldn't do to complain out here. Not when there's a practical solution in sight. Perhaps he simply needed some ice water or fresh air.

She tried to think of a way to diplomatically introduce the idea.

"Want to take a break and sit outside with me for a bit?" she asked, gesturing to the bench out front.

"I've got a pie in the oven," he said. "Hang on, let me check on it." He disappeared in the back, returning promptly. "Sure, I got a few minutes."

He lifted the bottom of his apron, mopping up his face with it, getting some flour on his cheeks. Then he used the tongs to transfer an oddly shaped mushroom of a bran muffin onto a small plate and handed it to Martha. His fingers left moist prints on the side, and Martha tried not to cringe.

Her fastidious nature wanted nothing more than to push the food away, give Terry a napkin to wipe his face, and leave. But one simply did not behave that way, not here. A small, shared community made you aware and accountable to others on a much more personal level. You didn't have to feel the same way, but you had to respect the feelings of other people.

She took the muffin and thanked him.

They stepped outside. Objectively speaking, it was perhaps hotter out on the bench, though the bakery's awning did its best to protect them from the worst of the sun. Martha was counting on the fresh air to do the trick.

"Are you hydrating enough in there?" she asked, picking at the muffin politely.

He shrugged with a smile, as if finding her sudden concern amusing.

"I keep thinking about that thing, you know," he said with a faraway look in his eyes. "The space ball. Like what are the odds of it finding us here? No one even really knows where we are, do they?" He rubbed his neck, cracking it from side to side. "Unless I guess that reporter knows now."

"She doesn't," Martha stated emphatically. "Measures were taken." She wasn't sure why she shared that. The information wasn't a secret, although it felt proprietary somehow.

"Well, there you go, then." Terry went on, unperturbed. "And this thing, small as it is, finds us. Could have hit anywhere, but it found us."

"The world is full of strange and random things," Martha said evenly.

"Not our world, though," Terry countered. "Our world out here is all about the opposite of strange and random, isn't it?"

He wiped the sweat out of his eyes with his sleeve. "Is your muffin okay?"

She forced herself to take a bite. It tasted off—salty?—but that could have just been psychological. "It's delicious, Terry, as always."

He smiled graciously. "Anyway, I keep thinking, what if it's some sort of a sign?" He looked at her questioningly, a bit embarrassed. "I mean, I'm so not that person, you know. Not superstitious, no woo-woo."

She knew that much. They prescreened for that. The island required dreamers and welcomed weirdos but shunned the wide-eyed and gullible. "They have to know how the world works at least enough to reject it," as Ronan had put it succinctly.

Terry had always struck her as the most practical of men. Now he was seeing signs.

"What do you mean?" she pushed gently. "A sign of what?"

He shrugged, his eyes to the skies. "Change?" he said, his voice quieter than usual, sweat pouring down his face.

Then he collapsed to the ground.

Martha, who seldom if ever raised her voice, didn't realize she was screaming until people came.

CHAPTER 9.
ARDEN.

"YOU KNOW WE were going to name the unicorns Franklin and Dewey originally," Ronan said casually.

"Right. The Dewey Decimal System." Arden nodded. "Makes sense."

"Except that we didn't," Ronan continued. "Because as it turned out, old Melvil Dewey was a real piece of work."

"Really?" Arden searched her brain and realized she didn't know the first thing about the man outside of his famous invention.

"Oh, yes. Rather famous for it. Sexist, racist, antisemitic. Quite unapologetic about all of it too. American Library Association went as far as to rename their top honor to get away from his name. No more Dewey medals."

"Wow, I had no idea."

Ronan turned to her and grinned. "His system is still in use, though. With his name on it and everything. Isn't it funny how selective we are about our outrage?"

"You mean, Rhonda uses that system in her library?"

"No." Ronan laughed and pushed his hair back. "Rhonda's got her very own system. She's the one who named the unicorns, too."

"Nice," Arden said noncommittally, sure there was more to come.

"What would you have done?" Ronan asked her, suddenly serious. "Would you have kept the name? After all, it was merely honoring the system, not the man himself?"

She sensed a test. Playful but undeniable. She had to think about her answer.

"Is there a separation between the man and his work?" she asked, replying with a question—a trick she stole from a therapist she used to see a while back.

Ronan sighed deeply. "I'd like to believe so," he said. "But I don't think the modern world can handle it. Everyone's much too self-righteous, too moralistic. The society at large seems to be veering into a form of neo-Puritanism, don't you find?"

"I thought I was here to ask the questions," she joked.

"Of course." He smiled, returning smoothly to his gracious host mode. "And here we are." He gestured around. "Behold the farm."

She looked, taking it all in. Neat. Pastoral. Bucolic. Not at all her thing, but she could appreciate how well it belonged here. No cattle, she noticed. Only goats, sheep, and chickens. They all looked well fed and taken care of, grazing happily. Or whatever passed for happiness in the animal kingdom.

Arden liked animals but in a largely abstract way; as in, she donated to an elephant rescue center in Kenya and dreamed of having a dog one day. But she'd never seen an elephant up close, and the dream of a dog was relegated to some distant future life, along with marriage and a house. In that moment, she wasn't sure if she was expected to go over there and pet them or ask any specific livestock questions, so she watched Ronan. And Ronan indeed did all those things. He petted a friendly goat, then approached the farm workers to chat with them.

Arden was introduced to Tyrone, a large, dark-skinned man with elaborate dreadlocks, and Lydia, a tall, thin woman with a deeply tanned, wrinkled face and sinewy arms. In her early fifties by Arden's estimation, she was likely at least a decade older than Tyrone. They didn't seem like an obvious couple, but once you watched them for a while, you saw how well they fit together: the unspoken grace of their union, the everyday dance of two people in love. There was a dog, too. An Australian shepherd named Flick for reasons no one explained.

Like everyone else on the island so far, Tyrone and Lydia seemed perfectly friendly. She asked them about their lives before coming here. Tyrone was a boxer, Lydia a literary agent. Jobs without meaning, they both agreed.

"And now?" Arden asked.

"Now it's easy," Tyrone replied, the more loquacious of the two of them. Lydia nodded along. "Life feels grounded, like every hour of every day makes sense. When I think back on what my life used to be, I can hardly believe it. I mean, what sort of person makes a living by beating the crap out of another person for the public amusement? It's . . ." He searched for a word.

"Barbaric," Lydia supplied.

"Exactly. See, right there, the evidence of brain damage," he joked.

Brain damage or not, he looked like he could bench press the livestock or carry the lot of them from one pasture to the next. Was that the appeal for Ronan? She was still figuring out his formula. But he was right. The people she met were all nice, good people—

the kind you'd want to be around. It made her mind tingle with suspicion. What were the odds?

Lydia told her she grew up on a farm. "I was Lainie back then," she said. "Didn't like it one bit. Wanted a big city life, a big city job. Got it all. Then spent years wondering why I was so unhappy."

'Did you figure it out?" Arden asked.

"I'm here, aren't I?" Lydia performed a complicated stretch, flexing her formidable arms. Tyrone noticed Arden look.

"It's yoga," he explained helpfully. "Lydia is our local yogi. I used to make fun of it as an exercise, but this woman's classes kick my butt."

Arden was skeptical of yoga herself. Too many of her friends swore by it, and she strongly suspected it was just so they could get away with wearing yoga pants outside. She had tried it before, following the trend, and didn't care for it. The meditation had failed to quiet her mind, and the practice had failed to challenge her body. But she had to admit, Lydia looked like she knew what she was doing.

"So you just went back to what you knew, what you grew up with? Farming? Is it really that simple? Is that the key to happiness?"

Lydia shrugged. "To each their own. If you're looking for some sort of magic happiness formula, you won't find it here."

"There is no formula," Tyrone seconded. "There is just a place where you are permitted to be your best self. Well, I suppose, you got to figure out what that self is first, but then you just, you know, go for it."

"Do you miss home?" Arden asked both of them, correcting it to "mainland" after they protested that they *were* home.

"I went back once," Tyrone told her. "Had to assist with a pickup, figured I'd see the sights and all."

"And? How was it?"

He pushed a hand across his face. "Loud. Dirty. Angry. I got racially profiled for waiting in an idling truck. I ate a greasy food truck taco that upset my stomach." He laughed uneasily. "Yeah, I couldn't wait to go back to the island at the end of that day."

Arden wanted to ask more, but Ronan had circled back to her after checking out the sheep and playing with the dog. He brushed some fur off his linen pants. "Ready to go?"

She picked up her cue. "Sure."

They said their goodbyes. Tyrone gave her a small log of goat cheese wrapped tightly in aluminum foil. "Freshly made."

"I don't know if I like goat cheese," she confessed to Ronan on their way out.

"Try it. It'll change your mind."

She did. It did. In one small bite there was a tangy, earthy flavor shot through with just enough sweetness. It tasted lighter and creamier than anything she'd had from cow's milk. She complimented the cheese, and Ronan threw up his hands, saying he couldn't take any credit for it.

"No cows, no beef. Don't you miss a good steak?" she asked him.

"I manage," he replied with a small smile.

"What's the one thing you do miss about the mainland?"

He cocked an eyebrow at her.

"Come on. There's got to be something," she pushed.

He was silent for a bit, long enough to make her think he wasn't going to answer, then he spoke.

"My place in the city had a skylight," he said. "I remember looking up at the night sky and never seeing any stars, only darkness. Because of all the light pollution. I'd watch that darkness, and it was strangely peaceful. But out here, there are always stars. And it feels like . . ." he paused, and Arden waited, "It feels like something is watching you back."

She wasn't sure what kind of an answer that was, only that it was simultaneously more and less than what she'd asked for.

The grass grew tall here, unmanicured, ungroomed to some inane regulations. It perfectly absorbed the sound of their footsteps. The strands of it reached to her ankles, and she idly wondered about ticks.

"You're from the East Coast originally?" he asked, observing her brush her hand at the bottoms of her jeans.

"Born and raised." She wouldn't be surprised if Martha had vetted her as thoroughly as any government agency prior to permitting this interview.

"I can tell. Jacob is too. Always worrying about ticks."

"Oh." She wondered if she blushed.

"It's okay," he told her. "You're safe here."

Ronan Bard was so easy to believe when he said things like that. She mentally regrouped.

"That story Tyrone told, about going back to the mainland for a visit."

Ronan smiled. "What about it?"

"Do you ever worry that people will get too, I don't know, soft living out here? That they'll lose their natural defenses? Or rather that their natural defenses will atrophy from disuse, and they'll no longer be able to fit in back on the mainland?"

He narrowed his eyes in thought. "But why would that even matter?"

"You don't think it would? For if and when they want to go back?"

She thought she saw his face darken a bit, but it could have just been a passing cloud momentarily obscuring the sun above them. "This isn't a summer camp, Arden," he said quietly, a note of caution in his voice.

Thin ice, she noted, but pushed on anyway. "Surely, you've had people leave before?"

"A few," he admitted. "Only a few."

"How come?"

"You'd have to ask them." He smiled openly, but she knew without a shadow of a doubt that anyone who left was probably bound by an NDA tighter than any straitjacket.

She wondered what it would take to leave this place. Or worse yet, get thrown out. What would it take to displease its smiling, magnanimous leader?

"So, this is forever?" she asked, keeping her tone light.

"Oh, no." Ronan shook his head, looking very serious. "Nothing is forever."

Those words stayed with Arden like a poorly digested meal, like a lead weight on her mind. She wasn't sure why. She didn't expect any particular permanency here. Or did she?

Back on the mainland, she was content to go through life as a renter, a borrower of living spaces, hearts, bodies. Use and be used and move on—that was the way of life. It was only cynical if you thought of it as such. Otherwise, it was just practical.

But out here, everything was so neat, so carefully crafted—a perfect dream of a place. It would be a shame if it simply ended.

What's more, everyone here seemed to be living this life like there was no end to it. The only person who had openly expressed his belief in this community's impermanence was its creator. Did the people here know? Would they care?

Ronan, after all, wasn't some temperamental authority figure. He was beloved. You could see it in the way people looked at and spoke of him.

Maybe forever was too big, too abstract of a concept to play around with. Maybe time—along with everything else—worked differently in this place. After all, today felt considerably longer than any other day. And they were just approaching lunch.

"Are you hungry?" Ronan asked as if reading her mind.

She nodded. "I could eat."

"Excellent," he said. "A fresh sourdough roll would go very well with that log of cheese. And you get to visit our bakery."

"I love bakeries," she said, clapping her hands together, changing the tone and mood of their conversation. "I bet a good bakery will bring you more interest than any piece of ideology alone."

"That's the idea," he said, joking along.

"Have you ever thought about tempering some of your views?" She just couldn't help herself. The man was like a Rubik's Cube: multifaceted, variegated, impossible, yet there was a feeling that with just the right twist you could get it all to line up and make sense.

"I've never thought of my views as particularly controversial," Ronan replied, spreading his arms, his face a picture of innocence.

"Seriously?" She arched her eyebrow at him.

"Seriously." He nodded, blond hair flopping boyishly into his eyes. "Give me a point, and I'll argue it. I've done my research. Everything I talk about is fact based and fact supported. I'm not some sort of an anti-establishment rebel, Arden." He pushed his hair back. "I'm simply the man who pointed out the establishment stopped making sense. And then offered an alternative."

She jotted it down mentally. All good, quotable material. She wished he wasn't so against recording devices. This day was certainly stretching the limits of her memory.

There was a small crowd gathered outside the bakery. A sign on the door.

Ronan found Martha, zeroed in on her. "What happened?" he asked, his voice perfectly calm. "Where's Terry?"

"He had some kind of an episode and passed out," she replied.

Arden thought the woman looked a bit harried, not as perfectly put together and businesslike as earlier that morning. Her hennaed hair was in a state of mild disarray.

"Did you take him to—?" Arden noted the concern in Ronan's voice.

"Of course." Martha seemed to remember herself now, brushing down her clothes and straightening out her hair. "I came back to lock up. I don't think anyone should be eating from the bakery until we know what's wrong with Terry. Just to be on the safe side."

Arden thought the woman looked pale, but that was understandable under the circumstances.

"Sure thing." Ronan smiled. "Folks, apologies, but as they say, better safe than sorry, right?"

Everyone dispersed, murmuring to themselves.

"I'd like to see inside," Ronan said, and Martha obliged, using the keys to let them in.

So they do use locks around here, Arden observed. *On special occasions.*

"You don't have to come in," Ronan suggested to her, which sounded more like, "Why don't you stay out here?"

It naturally made her want to go inside.

She split the difference by waiting in the doorway, eyeing the baked goods on display. They looked delicious but wrong somehow. It took a moment to realize it was the shape of them. Rather, the absence of conventional shapes on display. Was this the work of an eccentric baker, or someone about to, as Martha put it, "have an episode?"

There was no way to know.

She watched Ronan and Martha disappear into the back, then reappear, talking quietly to each other. She couldn't make out what they were saying, but it was impossible to ignore how out of sorts Martha looked. It made Arden think that perhaps her theory was right. Perhaps the people here had been too mellowed out by the easy life to comfortably face adversity. Though, she would have expected more of Martha. The woman seemed to have some steel in her.

The conversation was over. The two of them left the bakery, waiting for Arden to step out first, and locked the door once more.

"Arden, given the circumstances, perhaps a lunch at the café, instead?" Ronan said, like nothing happened.

"Will you be joining us?" Arden asked Martha.

"I think I've had too much excitement for one afternoon already," the older woman said. "Maybe another time."

She left, walking heavily toward what Arden presumed was her home. There were hardly any proper streets here, no city grids or anything of a sort, but none were needed. There was plenty to orient yourself.

An easily navigable space, Arden thought. She made a point of memorizing the phrase for her article.

"Shall we?" Ronan said, gesturing with his hand.

"Of course," she replied, and they walked the short distance to the café. She knew it wouldn't do to admit that seeing those oddly shaped pastries had completely killed her appetite.

After all, none of this was about the food. As they said amid the posh dining scene, it was all about the experience.

CHAPTER 10.
JACOB.

HE MOVED THROUGH his workday on willpower alone. His gut and his mind churned. There was a taste of blood in his mouth. He could only make out some of what Tony said to him.

They always had an easy banter despite their differences. Tony was a likable person, one of those rare individuals who retained their childlike wonder well into adulthood. He even looked the part with big blue eyes and a soft round face that hardly needed shaving. He was a true believer, a man powered by dreams. For him, the island had been the ultimate destination: his North Star and raison d'être.

There was a sort of single-mindedness to his pursuits that Jacob found refreshing. The man had worked in a big box store back on the mainland as a software technician, so he had always been a fan of tinkering with things. Only now it was less about computers and phones and more about things like small appliances, farm equipment, and bikes.

"What do you miss the most about your life before?" Jacob had asked him when they first started working together, feeling a mixture of protectiveness and curiosity about the younger newcomer.

"Video games," Tony replied instantly. "For sure."

"Why didn't you just bring some with you? I'm sure no one would mind."

Tony shifted from foot to foot. He wore an elaborate pair of basketball sneakers despite being no more than five and a half feet tall and not seeming athletic in the least.

"I would mind," he said quietly, seriously. "I've thought about it a lot. But back home, I mean, on the mainland," he corrected himself, "I was spending hours of my time every day gaming. And it was because I wanted an out, you know. Like my reality wasn't good enough, wasn't interesting enough, so I would just keep tuning into a fake one. And I don't want to do that anymore." He nodded with fierce determination. "I want to be fully present here."

Fully present sounded nice. It was one of those things Ronan said. Something about how the entertainment industry got dumber and dumber, pandering to the lowest common denominator by creating the greatest distance between the world it portrayed and the one people lived in. What else could explain the insane popularity of the Marvel Universe?

Ronan, a movie geek when he let it out, could go on and on about MU, and how—after all the false starts and sputters—it finally succeeded in the mid to late 2000s and never looked back. "Before all that," he'd say, "you have Superman movies, only some of which were good, and a bunch of random superhero offerings of varied but largely middling popularity. Why? Because the country was still by and large thriving, and people were fully engaged in it. But as years went on, things failed to improve—the wages stagnated, the politics got more and more unfathomable.

And people began to crave an ultimate departure from reality in their entertainment. The more powerless they felt, the more they needed superheroes on their screen."

And to everyone nodding along, Ronan would smile, almost bashfully, and add something like, "Sorry to go on, folks. My views may be out there, but that doesn't make them inaccurate."

The false modesty bit never quite took, in Jacob's opinion. He'd always wished he could have such strong opinions and such clear ways of expressing them. His anxiety alone wouldn't permit it. He passed out once, in high school, when he had to do a public presentation. Just dropped to the floor like a sack of potatoes, the typed preprepared speech crumpled in his sweaty hands.

"Jacob?" Tony's voice cut through his reverie. "Jacob, man, you okay?"

He blinked, forcing himself to focus on his immediate surroundings. Tony was standing before him, a concerned expression on his cherubic face.

"Yeah, sure," he forced the lie out.

"But . . ."

Jacob followed Tony's eyes to his hands. There was blood on them. Blood now on the bike wheel in front of him.

"I must have cut myself," he said, feeling lightheaded at the sight of his blood. There was something profoundly disturbing about seeing on the outside that which should remain inside.

"Why don't you go have Natalie bandage you up?" Tony suggested.

"No, no, I got this." Jacob pulled at his sleeves. "I'll take care of it."

"But what if you, like, need stitches or something? She can do that for you."

"I said I got it," Jacob snapped. The anger swept over him like a wave. He could have punched Tony in that moment. His bloody hands curled themselves into fists, and he shoved them in his pants pockets. "Fuck, you just don't listen," he spat out, forcing the boil of his blood to simmer.

Tony looked like he'd slapped him, a color rising high in his cheeks. "Sorry," he said uncertainly.

"I have to go," Jacob said. He had to put some distance between himself and others, at least until he got some rest and the itching had subsided. "Can you finish up on your own? Fetch Mox if you have to."

"Yeah, sure." Tony tried to smile, but the corners of his mouth wouldn't cooperate. "Whatever you need, man."

Jacob left before he could do or say anything else. The sun outside hit his eyes like raw onion, making them water. He pushed the tears away and walked, half-blinded, toward his house as quickly as he could. There was a lurch to the ground beneath his feet causing an unpleasant, vertiginous sensation.

Should he head toward the white building with the serpent twisting around the rod sign and let Natalie or one of her assistants help him? The instant gratification of being taken care of sounded tempting, but the demons riding his shoulders screamed at him to get home, lock the door, curl into a ball, and contain his crumbling inner world himself.

The passersby were blurry shapes, the sky an overzealous spotlight above him as Jacob finally made his way to the familiar shape of his house. He got inside and engaged the lock, then lowered the window blinds.

At last he could do the thing he'd been dying to do. The thing he'd been terrified to do. Jacob took off his clothes and looked at his body. The rash was everywhere now, everywhere he could see. Just as angry, just as bright red as the rage oscillating within him. His arms were deeply scratched by the bike's spokes, weeping blood down his wrists. It looked like a botched suicide attempt.

A bath, he thought. Something with oatmeal in it to soothe the skin. He had never done that before, but somehow it seemed right.

He put a stopper into the bathtub's drain and started the water. From the kitchen, he fetched a container of oatmeal. It was about a third full. Unsure of how much to use, he ended up dumping the entire thing into the water, then stirred it around with his hand. The water was turning light pink, he noticed. It took a moment to realize it was from his blood.

When the tub was half full, he climbed in. It was lukewarm, so he turned up the hot water, setting in, waiting for the oatmeal to do its trick. The pale sodden flakes of it were congealing all around him into something paste-like. He began applying it to his skin. His hands shook, he saw, but then he'd never been good with blood.

He thought about how rude he'd been to Tony and flinched. He'd never spoken to the younger man like that before, never. It was like kicking a puppy.

Jacob scrubbed his hands with a soap bar until they were free of blood, everywhere but the thin dark rings around his fingernails usually reserved for things like bike grease. Then he washed his face.

He couldn't tell if the bath was working. Maybe? He felt a bit calmer. Suddenly he remembered a book he had. A plant guide.

He got out of the tub and, dripping water everywhere, walked to the bookshelf in the living room and pulled out an old hardcover book in a tattered dust jacket. He retraced his steps and stepped back into the tub, taking care to keep his hands dry.

The book was old. Probably a gift, but he couldn't remember right now. Checking the index in the back, he paged to the entry on poison ivy.

The letters blurred in front of his eyes, but he wasn't going to go looking for his reading glasses so he squinted to focus.

It was geographically specific, for one thing, poison ivy. Also, it caused blisters. He didn't see any on him, but that didn't mean they weren't there. For the first time, Jacob wished he had a full-size mirror. Instead, he settled for putting the book down and tentatively feeling along his back with his fingers, stretching as far as his arms could reach. He then dried his hands on the towel and picked the book back up. According to the entry, it wasn't all that dangerous generally. He was likely having an extreme reaction. Or whatever he was reacting to wasn't actually poison ivy. But that would mean—

The panic seized him so tightly that he dropped the book to the floor. What if it *was* that stupid space ball? What if it brought with it some kind of space toxins? But he was hardly near it. Terry was the one who carried it. He should check in with Terry.

Jacob stood up, water and sodden oatmeal paste dripping off of him. He toweled off gently and put on the softest clothes he could find: an old tattered and faded T-shirt and shorts he used as pajamas. He slipped his feet into a worn pair of sneakers and stepped outside. Sunglasses. He popped back in to get a pair. Now he was ready. He just had to make his way to the bakery.

His head felt like someone was holding drumming auditions inside it. The thought of interaction, any interaction, suddenly seemed unfathomable. His feet turned and, as of their own volition, carried him to the beach instead. A short walk and the ground turned to warm sand. He kicked off his shoes.

BEAUTIFUL, ONCE

Jacob had always loved the ocean, but living by the beach was a financial impossibility back on the mainland. Here, in paradise, it was always only a short walk away. When the wind obliged, carrying the sound into his bedroom through the open window, Jacob would fall asleep listening to the sound of gently rolling waves.

There was a danger living like this, he knew, surrounded by water, in a world of rising sea levels, but morbid as it was, he couldn't think of a better way to go.

Humanity came from the sea. It was only poetic to return to it.

There were a few people on the beach, but it was mostly empty. Jacob made a beeline for the water, without bothering to shed his clothes. He felt the water-flattened sand beneath his feet, then the waves softly lapping at his skin: ankles, knees, waist, arms. He didn't stop until he was in up to his chin.

The way the salt water ignited his skin was like walking into fire, setting the damage there alight, yet he couldn't stop himself. It felt pure or purifying in a profound way. He didn't know how long he stood there. The burning sensation eclipsed all other thoughts, all other feelings, and there was peace in that.

Eventually, Jacob took a deep breath and put his head underwater. His sunglasses swam away. He noted it with distant regret; he'd had the same pair of Wayfarer knockoffs for years.

He'd half expected to see fire underwater, but there was nothing like that. Only his own limbs distorted by the watery perspective, only the ocean floor and all the things found there. An ecosystem of its own. Another world.

And something else. A pair of legs? The legs were attached to a body. He recognized Patrick Wong—one of Natalie's assistants and a surfer in his time off—a short, muscular man with long dark hair tied up in a bun. A hand was grabbing Jacob's shoulders, lifting him up until both their heads were above water.

"Hey, bro, are you okay?" Patrick's broad, friendly face swam in and out of Jacob's vision. "You were under for quite a bit."

Jacob opened his mouth. He wanted to thank the man for his concern, to tell him he was A-OK, to ask to be left alone. But none of the words came out. It was almost as if he had forgotten how to form them.

Instead, to his great, uncomprehending horror, he lunged for the man. There was screaming, and a salty, metallic taste flooding his mouth. He thought he was drinking the seawater, but everything was red, so red.

Jacob pushed off, blinking to clear his vision. Patrick Wong's eyes were huge and full of fear. There was a jagged wound on his neck weeping red tears. Like an animal bite. Patrick was desperately trying to staunch the blood flow with his hands, but it wasn't enough. The blood kept seeping through his fingers. His feet were moving, either treading water or spasming. Or perhaps trying to get away from his attacker.

Jacob's first instinct was to help. He reached for the wounded man. Patrick tried to scream but only got a mouthful of water for his trouble. Were his vocal cords severed?

Jacob's second instinct was to finish the job. This proved to be so much easier to accomplish.

He heard voices from the shore, calling after Patrick. Not yet alarmed, merely concerned. *I should talk to them,* Jacob thought, and his body began moving as if of its own accord.

He walked through fire engulfing him, back toward the shore, leaving the ruined man behind. They were running to meet him, running through the water. The two of them, a young woman and her friend. Patrick's friends, he told himself, trying to make sense of it all. They came to the island for the ocean. To surf their days away. Patrick was putting his EMT training to good use working with Natalie. His girlfriend—what was her name? Jacob could not remember—did something with art? Taught art? And her friend? He couldn't think at all.

Suddenly, they were in his arms. A strange and awkward hug that went on and on. Jacob could see the fire transferring from his skin to theirs. And he was thirsty, so thirsty. All that salt he had drunk. He just needed something, anything to moisten his lips. So that he could speak, so that he could explain.

But they were going limp in his arms now, like marionettes with their strings cut. Lifeless.

Jacob let them go and continued toward the shore until he felt the sand scorch his feet. There were a few more people. He blinked and blinked, but he could not make out their faces through the reddish haze.

They can help, he thought. There was no reason to be afraid anymore. Safety in numbers. His body felt so strange, so foreign and unwieldy. And that sun, was it always so bright? Where were his sunglasses? Did they melt in the fire?

Jacob could see the flames traveling up and down his arms. It looked beautiful. The people standing before him were staring at him. Could they see it too?

He'd been so many things over the years, most of them disappointing. He'd come here, to the island, to learn to be himself. What was he now? Had he become something new?

He reached for the people in front of him, a modern Prometheus, his arms outstretched. "Here," he told them. "I have brought you fire."

CHAPTER 11.
MARTHA.

SHE WENT WITH HIM at first because it was the right thing to do. A decent thing to do, at any rate. Or perhaps she went with him because she was in shock. It was difficult to tell and ultimately didn't seem to matter much.

Whatever the reasons were, they brought her back here, to be by his side. She had done the responsible thing by putting up the sign, locking up the bakery, and telling Ronan what was going on. And then she returned to this somber, sterile space without even thinking about it.

Now she was here, sitting by Terry's bed, in a room with too much white in it, studying his face. He seemed peaceful for the moment. Natalie had diagnosed him with acute dehydration so he'd been hooked up to a drip line. No one seemed particularly concerned, which Martha took to be a good sign, but Natalie still drew Terry's blood for tests.

Off-the-grid or not, the facilities on the island were as modern as anywhere on the mainland, and if there was something Natalie and her team couldn't do, Ronan had a helicopter service on standby. The idea was for people to feel safe and taken care of here, and it had worked perfectly thus far. No complaints.

For all his controversial views on the healing of the mind, Ronan was a firm believer in healing the body—another paradox from a man full of them.

Martha could still recall the things Ronan had said about psychology over the years. He'd never come out and slammed it as quack science or anything like that, but he was skeptical at best.

"It's a sign of a declining society," he'd said, "that we should develop such dependency on talking to strangers. As the social fabric that binds us erodes, as communities fail to provide communal spirit, people are left feeling more and more isolated, misunderstood, left out. So much so that they are willing to spend hundreds of dollars per hour to have a perfect stranger listen to them. Our world makes its citizens feel unheard, and instead of bellowing their discontent out loud, they have learned to share it quietly, privately, with those paid to hear it."

"What about people with serious mental problems who need help?" the interviewer had asked Ronan, looking properly aghast.

"That's psychiatry." Ronan raised his eyebrow, a small smile playing on his lips. Match set and won. "A different science altogether. A proper science. One that has my full support."

Martha still remembered the controversy that interview had caused, and the conversation they had afterward.

"Would it kill you—" she began with a sigh.

"What if it did?" He threw back with a smirk. "And the last thing I said was a lie? What would that do to my soul? Would it make it heavier than a feather?"

Martha recognized the Egyptian mythology reference. She'd

read about Ma'at and her brand of truth, wrapped in harmony. She'd been trying to keep up with Ronan's esotericism.

Sometimes she couldn't tell if he was a genius or a madman, or if there was a difference. The things he said made it difficult to gauge whether he meant them sincerely or was merely courting controversy. He swore it was the former, and she chose to go with that despite what her innately skeptical nature might have suspected.

Skepticism was heavy. All the things Martha had carried through life, all her dark clouds, they weighed her down. She wanted to leave it all behind on the mainland, to start anew on the island. To an extent, she did. The "wherever you go, there you are" adage proved all too applicable; still, the time she had spent by Ronan's side, here on the island, had been the happiest of her life.

As far as she could tell, it was worth everything.

Terry shifted, bringing Martha out of her thoughts and back to reality. She was lightly nauseous, which she attributed to stress and the uncomfortable environment. The sterile smell gave her the heebie-jeebies because it reminded her of watching her grandfather die when she was a child. The old man had looked like a pile of sticks strewn under a white sheet, his face skeletal, eyes watery. He had never remembered who she was until the very end. His eyes opened wide as if something had been peering through them from another place. Martha felt seen, recognized, and terrified of it. She ran out of his room, shaking, and refused to go back in. The next day, her grandfather died.

Terry, on the other hand, looked as robust as ever, though his pallor left something to be desired. Martha was embarrassed by her screaming earlier. The man had simply fainted. She didn't need to make such a production of it. All she had to do was summon help. The screaming worked well enough for that purpose; still, she hated the thought of losing her composure in front of others.

"Terry?" she said softly, leaning in. "Terry?"

Something shifted beneath his features, like an expression trying to form. Perhaps he was coming to.

What did she know about the man besides words on paper? He scored well on personality tests, particularly high on cooperation and friendliness. Pretty good on adaptability, too. He had a family once, but too long ago to matter. He used to work in construction which damaged his hearing. He'd been happy as a baker here on the island. He was a considerate neighbor. A jolly, friendly man. A peculiar dresser, favoring inexplicable color combinations.

There had to be more. Martha thought about it.

He played the harmonica on his porch and now and again for their impromptu concerts and talent shows. He wasn't a stranger to marijuana. He was a wild and wildly amusing dancer, surprisingly light on his feet for a man his size.

How well could you know someone from the outside looking in? Having spent most of her life feeling unseen and unknown by others, Martha couldn't be sure. The kaleidoscopes within each and every person—the colors, shapes, and emotions held within, anything beyond the comprehensible data and easily acquired surface knowledge—remained a mystery.

Easier for a deity to put a heart on a scale against a feather and judge it than leave it to mortals. A simple practical solution for a complex problem. No wonder Ronan was a fan.

Covetousness was the most egregious of sins in Ancient Egypt, Martha remembered, for it had encouraged selfishness, self-pity, jealousy, and worst of all, displayed an absence of gratitude for the gifts bestowed. It made the heart too heavy to pass the test, and its bearer unable to proceed to paradise.

Ronan had a lot to say about that too, of course. And Martha agreed with him on it, one hundred percent. He spoke of how the society encouraged covetousness, how it catered to blind desire and championed greed as a value. How it measured success in money and possessions acquired with it, making everyone clamor for more, more, more at all costs.

It was easier on the island. No more of the never-ending chase for more. Here, there was only enough, and the fine appreciation of enough. Epicurus, one of Ronan's favorite philosophers with his constant advocacy of moderation, would have been proud.

Terry moaned. She couldn't tell if it was in discomfort or not. Reluctantly, Martha leaned over and took his hand. It felt large, heavy, and clammy. She wanted to drop it immediately but held on as a concession to her better angels. The weight of it made her think of a slab of meat, not part of a person.

Suddenly, Terry opened his eyes. The motion seemed puppeteered, as if someone had reached inside the man's skull and flicked his eyelids open like window shutters. In his gaze, Martha saw the thing she'd only ever seen in her dying grandfather's eyes. That same hungry, searching darkness. She wanted to back away, but Terry's hand, the one she was holding, was suddenly insistently agile. It squeezed her hand tightly, his fingers locking around it like meaty snares.

Don't scream, Martha told herself. *Do not scream again.* She wasn't *that* person. She wasn't some hysterical woman cliché.

"Terry," she said, forcing calmness into her tone. "You're awake. Let me call Natalie."

He blinked once, twice. "I'm sorry," he said, his voice caught between a whisper and a croak. "I'm so sorry."

"For what?" she asked, thinking the man delirious.

"This," he replied, his voice shifting to a terrible growl, as he lunged at her like a predator awakened.

CHAPTER 12.
ARDEN.

THE SMELL HIT her first, charmed her, lured her in. Warm cinnamon, toast, and something else, something that made her think of her childhood. If the café could bottle it up and sell it as perfume or candles, they'd make a fortune.

Then again, Arden didn't think any of these people were particularly interested in money. In fact, she decided to talk to Ronan about it now as they waited for their food at a cutesy table by the window. Everything was decorated here and seemingly by different people. The overall theme was whimsy with a hint of boho chic, which worked well with mismatched pieces.

Ingrid, the woman who ran the café, was tall and angular, with long blonde hair pulled back into a ponytail. On TV, she'd play a Scandinavian cop or a Viking's wife. In reality, she was married to Rory, a small bear of a man as hirsute as he was friendly. He didn't speak, either biological or elective mutism, but it didn't seem to matter. There was such warmth in his eyes, especially when he looked at Ingrid. And apparently, he was an absolute wizard in the kitchen.

"Think of a meal, and Rory will make it," Ronan boasted with a laugh. But Arden, still not hungry after seeing those horrid pastries, opted for the simplest thing she could think of: the sourdough roll Ronan had boasted for her goat cheese.

"Nothing else?"

"No, thank you."

Ronan shook his head with mock disappointment and asked for the soup du jour and a quinoa bowl.

Is that how he eats to stay in such amazing shape or is it all part of the show? Making a good impression for company? Arden wondered.

"I'd probably demolish a personal-size pizza if I was here by myself," he confessed as if reading her mind. "Martha always says that left to my own devices, I'd eat like a kid."

Or an adult with a perfect metabolism, Arden thought cynically. *Some of us have to work to stay thin.*

"So, how does it work here on the island?" she said, plunging in after taking a sip of cucumber-flavored water. "Is it basically socialism?"

He pushed his hair back and smiled. "Depends on your definition."

"Oh, you know, the garden variety. Social ownership, collectivism, community rule. 'From each according to his ability, to each according to his needs,' and all that."

"I love that you can casually quote Marx," he told her, smiling.

"But it doesn't answer my question," she pointed out.

He held up his hands. "Sure, yeah, you got me. I suppose in the broadest sense our structure is close to socialism. With one notable difference."

Arden arched her eyebrow.

He grinned. "Ours works."

"But that could simply be down to timing, no?" Arden countered.

"How so?"

"You haven't been out here long enough to see it fail yet," she elaborated. "Historically speaking, socialism failed in every place that has ever tried it."

"Socialism failed in every *country* that has ever tried it," he corrected, his banter-like tone friendly. "It's the same thing as with most good ideas. You can't sustain it with a large population."

"As opposed to a small, curated population?"

He grinned broader. "Exactly."

Rory glided to their table as silent as a ninja, depositing their food then disappearing. It smelled amazing. Arden forced herself to focus.

"So, what you're saying is that the majority of the population across the world is too stupid for its own good?"

Ronan frowned comedically at her. "Arden, you know fully well that I said no such thing."

"It was implied."

He stirred his soup, watching a small cloud of steam rise. She watched his face intently, waiting for that small, telltale shift when the interviewee decided to go off script. After all, going off script was something of Ronan's specialty. She didn't catch it, that mischievous narrowing of the eyes, the decisive thinning of the lips.

He simply looked up at her and said, "Yes, most people are stupid. Worse, they are ignorant. Cruel, small-minded, hateful. Most people have never met a good idea they didn't want to destroy or a brilliant mind they didn't want to set on fire. They lead dull lives and die dull deaths with nothing of note in between." He tilted his head a bit to the side as if studying her. "But you already know all this, don't you? Because you, Arden, are not like most people."

Wow, she thought. *He's good. He's really good.* The way he was looking at her just then sent shivers down her spine. Like she had been seen. Truly seen. And selected for greatness.

That was how he did it, wasn't it? How he got these people here? Into his cult or whatever it was. To be considered like that and found worthy: more than that—special. It could make a believer out of anyone.

"I think I'm rather ordinary," she said modestly.

Ronan quirked his lips in amusement and took a sip of his soup, followed by a forkful from his quinoa bowl.

She followed suit, picking up the goat cheese sandwich she had made and biting into it. The roll, generously buttered and lightly browned, complemented the cheese perfectly. It was as good a sandwich as she had ever had and better than most. She was suddenly hungry, ravenous for it; she didn't want it to end.

"Do you know how many interview requests I get?" Ronan asked her finally, dabbing a linen napkin to his lips.

"A lot?" she guessed.

"That's right," he said simply. Not bragging, merely stating the fact. "And I chose to speak with you."

Was there too much weight on the word "chose?" She couldn't tell.

The café played music she did not recognize, strange percussion and lyrics she could not understand.

"Because I'm special?" she joked.

"Self-deprecation doesn't suit you," he said. "It doesn't suit anyone, really. You should be your biggest fan."

"Do you mean *your* biggest fan?" Arden wondered if that was a push too far.

Ronan simply shook his head. "How's your sandwich?"

"Excellent. How's your soup?"

"Excellent." He beamed her a genuine smile. "I can only hope one day my ideas will be as universally beloved as Rory and Ingrid's food."

"Aren't they?"

Ronan guffawed. "I've always thought of myself as more of an acquired taste."

Arden finished her sandwich and wiped her lips with a napkin, wishing for more food. "Do you believe everything you say?" she asked, plunging right in. "Many regard you as a sort of agent provocateur, someone all too happy upsetting the prevalent zeitgeist for a personal statement."

Ronan put his spoon down and steepled his fingers under his chin. "Do people still think that?"

"Sure, yes. You have to agree, you're rather controversial. The immigration thing alone . . ."

He waved it off. "I've said plenty more controversial things before and after everyone got so hung up on immigration."

"Aren't you a great-grandson of immigrants?" Arden asked pointedly.

"Everything has its place and time," he replied, picking his spoon back up. "My ancestors came to a young nation that required more population, labor, and expertise."

"And now?"

"And now, it is a struggling nation, failing to take care of its own." He tilted the soup bowl away from him to finish it, the proper way. "Aren't you bored of this? Why don't we talk about something—anything—else?"

"Sure." She took a sip of water, feeling like she had pushed him as far as she safely could.

Truth be told, she still didn't know what to think. For all their talking, Ronan stubbornly remained an enigma. She couldn't tell how much of what he presented was performative. Was he the visionary some thought he was? A man who understood the system well enough to know how to rig it for a win? Was he someone who stepped outside the bounds of convention far enough to see that it was all built to break those invited to participate? Was he a visionary who saw the faults of the old world order and founded a new one?

Was he right? Was this small, insular living a better alternative?

Back on the mainland, she would have likely proclaimed him a lunatic, a fanatic, a man spoiled enough by good fortune to dare play God.

Here, in his world, seeing it from the inside, she could understand all too well the seductive power of this life—of Ronan himself.

Could she stay here? More importantly, what would she miss from her old life if she did?

This food and music were too relaxing. Arden could feel her mind drifting. She could take a nap. Process everything slowly, at her own pace. But time wasn't on her side, and so she pushed on.

"Could we talk a bit more about the lost years?"

"It still amuses me to hear a part of my life referred to that way," he said, shaking his head.

"What would you prefer?"

"I'd prefer people didn't call it anything."

"But they do," she insisted. "You want to be legendary, you've got to have a legend. And those tend to come with chapters."

He nodded solemnly, finishing his quinoa bowl without much enthusiasm.

"What would you call it?" She changed tactics. "In your autobiography, how would you describe the time after your tech success and before the island?"

It was years; he was gone from the public eye for years. Nothing but rumors and speculation. A vanishing unlike any other. For someone of Ronan's public status, virtually unheard of.

Arden had heard it all and revisited it all while preparing for this interview: an off-grid passionate love affair gone wrong, a stint as a masked professional wrestler, a sojourn in a Buddhist monastery, time spent orbiting the Earth. The latter theory was particularly popular due to Ronan's well-publicized obsession with space. Before his disappearance, the man had, at one point, almost single-handedly saved NASA from financial insolvency. They named a rover and the latest in the line of potentially habitable planets after him. Bard this, Bard that. Bard the planet had promise, but so did many places that turned out to be nothing. Some said it wasn't a planet at all. The skeptics referred to it as the "future Pluto."

Ronan, a contradiction in all matters, wasn't among these skeptics. Despite his sobering, pessimistic look at humanity at large, when he turned his gaze to the skies there were stars in his eyes. Arden had watched some of his interviews from back then. The NASA thing was heavily publicized, and Ronan always had a lot to say on the subject of the cosmos. But he stopped talking about that too. In the end, there was nothing important enough to pull his attention away from the island.

Still, Arden figured she wouldn't put it past him to have snuck away into outer space for a while. She could just see him, the man on the moon, casting a judging eye to the blue marble in the distance and finding it wanting. Years were a long time for someone, *anyone*, to be away, wherever away may be. And people seldom came back the same.

The sound of the café's door opening and closing brought Arden back to the present moment.

Ronan looked out of the window, his expression unreadable. He slowly turned back to face her. "I would describe them as the best years of my life," he said, simply, seriously.

It was a perfect answer, one so much bigger than the question. It spoke volumes.

For a moment, Arden saw a crack in his golden boy façade, a glimmer of a man as sad and lost as the rest of them, but better at hiding it. Then the moment passed, like a cloud unveiling the sun again, blinding her with its brightness. Ronan smiled and asked if she'd like to order dessert.

She said yes, if only to keep the momentum going, but also because she genuinely wanted more food, specifically the pie in the front display with a calligraphic tag proclaiming it to be Pecan Passion. She hadn't felt passionate about food for some time, having never been much of a cook. Chris was fine with takeout when they ate together. The kitchen of his condo remained as immaculately unused as hers. By and large, food had been fuel to Arden, something often consumed on the go or in front of the TV. When she went out to eat, it was mostly to socialize or talk business, the textures and flavors on the plate before her sat wasted, losing priority to the conversation.

But here on the island, life was just slow enough to pause and give in to culinary delights—just slow enough to develop a passion for pecan.

Ronan ordered her a slice.

"You don't want one?" she asked self-consciously.

"I'd probably burst if I did," he joked, "but I'll still likely steal a bit of yours."

"Could you tell me more about that time?"

He chewed his lip, looking boyish, tilting his head down to look up at her, a touch of a winsome charm. She could only imagine how many tough spots that look had gotten him out of.

"Come on. You can't just say 'the best years of your life' and not elaborate," she prodded. "You gotta give me something."

He sighed and rubbed his neck. "I had this idea," he finally said, "of an infinite and benevolent universe. And me, a citizen of it."

Ah, there it is, Arden thought as she smiled to herself. *A casual confession. Look how big he dreamed before scaling down.*

"Sure," Arden offered. "It's a tempting idea."

He looked down at his hands. "You could say I tried reaching out."

"Oh my God." She didn't mean to say it out loud, it just came out. "So, the golden record thing is true?"

One of the wildest rumors about Ronan Bard was that he created a golden record on par with the ones Voyager spacecrafts carried to space in the late seventies and sent out into the universe. He certainly had the money and hubris to do it.

There were stranger things out there that people did with their money. Stranger things they've sent into space, too, like the ashes of their loved ones. But something about a private golden record didn't sit the right way with the public opinion.

Perhaps because the original records carried what many thought were the best of humanity: its sounds, its accomplishments, its dreams. What would Ronan's say? And did it mean that he thought of himself as the best humanity had to offer?

Showmanship and arrogance, long admired in modern politics, didn't quite translate outside of the field, it seemed. But it was only a rumor, wasn't it?

Ronan looked at her, mildly amused.

"You did it, didn't you? Just like NASA did?"

"No, Arden. Not like NASA." Ronan laughed. Her pecan pie arrived, and he reached out to steal the tip of it with his fork. "If I were to do such a thing, I would have done it very, very differently."

"How so?" she inquired. The pie melted in her mouth. Yes, this was the thing to make one passionate about pecans, about life itself. She could swoon, but it wouldn't do. Instead, she caught Rory's eye and gave him a thumbs up. It seemed dorky but appropriate. Rory grinned or so she thought—there was too much facial hair to tell for sure—and disappeared behind the counter.

"Well, how much do you know about the original records?" Ronan asked, licking a stray pie flake off his lips.

"Um." She had to dig around her memory, unprepared to be quizzed and all too mellowed out by the dessert. "There were two of them, sent out on Voyagers. Recordings and pictures meant to represent us as a species. I think Carl Sagan was involved."

"Very good." Ronan grinned approvingly like she had passed the test. "Just one more thing. They were sent out without a destination in mind. Just . . . space. They've left the solar system some time ago, and they are still out there." He waved his hand nebulously. "Just floating around in some interstellar darkness."

"Right, yes." She finished her pie and drank some water.

"So you wouldn't do it with any other important piece of mail, would you?" He drummed his fingers on the table. "You wouldn't just take the 'message in a bottle' approach with something so valuable?"

"Well, sure," Arden started tentatively, "but it wasn't like they had an address."

"No, they did not," Ronan exclaimed emphatically. "Just hope and good intentions."

"Okay," she said slowly. "So how would you do it? In theory, of course."

"In theory, of course," he began before getting cut off by a loud clanging din. It took Arden a moment to recognize it as the sound of a bell ringing. She had seen it on their walk but took it to be decorative, rather like the Liberty Bell in Philadelphia, only intact. She hadn't expected it to actually ring. Or for that ringing to be quite so distressingly piercing.

"What the hell?" she said, acutely aware of the alarm stirring itself awake at the pit of her stomach, from somewhere beneath the cheese and the pie.

Ronan was already getting up. "I'm afraid we have to cut this short, Arden," he said in a tone that brooked no argument. "I have to go."

He left, moving quickly, purposefully, though not running. Like a good leader, the man knew it wouldn't do to show panic. And like a good journalist, sensing that the story was about to get a lot more exciting, Arden followed.

CHAPTER 13.

JACOB.

H E'D ALWAYS BEEN good at fixing things. Somehow, instinctively he just knew how the pieces were supposed to fit together. It was his gift. Jacob had always believed it was what ultimately got him his spot on the island.

If there was one fact you could rely on in an uncertain world, it was this—things got broken. You always needed someone to come along and put them back together. Jacob hadn't done much with his life besides making a mess of it. But here, given a second chance, he'd been happy repairing the damage in whatever form it found.

He could fix this too, he thought. This messy puzzle of broken bodies and torn limbs. He just had to think.

The sun was beating down on him like a hammer: relentless, powerful. His skin felt sticky. The blood drying upon it was turning into a reddish-brownish film. The sweat pouring down his face kept melting some of it into his eyes. He kept wiping at it with his forearm.

Oddly enough, he felt perfectly calm. All the fear, all the anxiety had left him now. There was only peace, though he wasn't sure why that should be.

The dead bodies around him didn't look quite real. Jacob felt like he had stepped into a still frame of some violent video game or a movie. He knew it wasn't a dream—there were too many somatic sensations for that—but it didn't quite strike him as reality either.

The body parts around him—he just had to think of them as any other components of any other machinery. Gather the parts, find the pattern, fix it. Fix this!

His legs were all pins and needles as if they'd fallen asleep, affecting his walking and balance. Staggering, he began to collect the body parts. They were heavy, so heavy.

He was thirsty again. Why didn't anyone have water? Who comes to the beach without water?

He looked around. Something wasn't quite right. Time moved around him in clicks like images shuffled through an old-fashioned slide projector. With missing moments in between.

Jacob was no stranger to blackouts, having lost plenty of time back on the mainland to benzos and booze, particularly when he mixed and matched. This was different, and he didn't know what to make of it.

Beneath the unforgiving sun, with limbs that now felt like bags of sand and sand that felt like molten lava on his skin, Jacob worked to put together all he had torn asunder.

Time skipped. Frame after frame.

Flip and he was drinking, but where did the water come from? Flip, and he was trying to match the legs to the torso. Flip, and he was wiping at his mouth, his hand coming away as blood red as the rest of him. Flip, and he was struggling to put innards back into someone's stomach. Flip, flip, flip.

He was ravenous now. And he didn't think he was making

much progress. Usually, he would have fixed it by now, but this project refused to come together. He was tired of it, but not ready to give up. His work was the only thing he'd ever been stubborn about—you didn't leave things half done. He simply needed a break. He'd grab a bite to eat, a drink, and come back to finish.

Jacob hated the idea of leaving a mess behind. The sand was littered. He did not litter. He left each place he inhabited in the same or better shape than he had found it, the way everyone did on the island. Their campground rule, their motto.

He studied the pattern of blood on the sand for a while, the dried swirls of it on his hands. He should wash up, he was right near the water. But it felt far. The sun, reflected off its surface, blinded him.

He'd just have to get some sustenance, that's all. Everything made better sense on a full stomach. Granted, the way his stomach was growling made it seem like it might never be full again, but how could that be possible? Surely any appetite could be sated.

Jacob made a pile of the ruined bodies, arranging them as neatly as he could, then slowly, so slowly began walking toward the island's center.

The fragmented time all around him must have sped up the trip, for it would have felt inordinately slow otherwise. Eventually, he saw people. An enormous relief flooded him, coursing through his veins like the finest vodka. Like fire.

They came at him in movie frames, one after another. Each face a picture of concern, shock, horror. It made him feel dizzy, disoriented.

He looked around for something to anchor him and spotted the bell. It was the centerpiece of the small park in what qualified as the island's main street. A symbolic object but also a functional one. It was meant to be rung for happy occasions and as a distress signal, but it turned out to be too clamorous of a thing and thus stayed largely decorative.

There were benches in the park. Jacob sat down for a moment, just to gather his thoughts. Someone reached out for him. He thought he heard his name being said.

Flip frame: he reached back toward the person. Flip frame: he was drinking, he was eating. Did they give him water? Did they give him food? So kind, it was so kind.

The next thing he heard was a noise so terrible, it brought him to his knees. Above the screams—why was everyone screaming?—he recognized the clanging of the bell. It wasn't resonant, and it wasn't melodious like the bells of the church he lived near as a kid. This sound felt like it was reaching right into his head and tearing at his brain. Yet it called him somewhere he did not want to go.

He had to stop it. Stop it now. Jacob tried standing up, fell over, and proceeded to crawl toward the bell, his progress impossibly slow, despite the temporal skips.

A person was standing there, ringing it, their eyes on Jacob, their face a blur. He blinked the blood and sweat out of his eyes, but the blurring effect remained. Who was this? A stranger?

There shouldn't have been any strangers on the island. That wasn't right. The figure stretched and wavered in front of him. Was it even human?

Summoning all his remaining strength, Jacob leaped up to stop the monster at the bell. They both fell to the ground in a tangle of limbs. There was a cry. Or was it a growl?

It didn't matter. The bell had to be stopped. Jacob reached for it, steadying the clamoring part with his shaky, bloody hand. What was the name of it, this ringing bit? Something funny. The culler? The clapper, that's it.

"The clapper," he tried to tell everyone, but he was too parched to speak. He fell to the ground beneath the bell, staring into the darkness of its hollow chamber, and the darkness stared back.

CHAPTER 14.
MARTHA.

SHE WAS SAVED by Natalie's assistant, Jasper, who pulled Terry off her and sedated the man. Now that she'd been patched up, the scratches Terry left on her skin—bruises certain to emerge any moment—didn't seem to matter as much as the shock.

Martha had been offered something for it, but she wasn't sure she wanted the feeling to go away. It was more like she wanted to sit with it, examine it, try to understand it.

Terry had been strapped to bed with improvised belt restraints. Though he was unconscious, Martha could see his eyes flickering beneath their lids, making her imagine strange creatures trapped in membranous cocoons, waiting to burst out. Was he dreaming? What was he dreaming?

Attacking someone didn't seem like a normal side effect, no matter how extreme the dehydration.

Natalie posited Terry may have been hallucinating, which seemed plausible in theory, but she didn't see his eyes when he lunged. No, Martha was the only one who saw them, and she was sure without a shadow of a doubt, her attacker knew exactly what he was doing. The only thing she wasn't sure of was who lunged at her, who peered at her through Terrence Cauley's eyes. It wasn't her neighbor, the jolly local baker she'd been friendly with for years, the man who could make something as shrill as the harmonica sound palatable. No, it was definitely someone else.

So here she was, watching him, waiting to be proven right.

Because she was seldom if ever wrong, and also because she felt much too tired to go on about her day or even go home. All her limbs felt terribly heavy, and she wondered if it was the shock of all that had happened working its way through and out of her system.

The violence would have jarred her even back on the mainland, but out here, in this oasis of peace and calm, it was unthinkable. Impossible.

Once, a long time ago, she had been threatened by an irate parent of an unruly pupil she had elected to expel. She could feel it coming: the way the color kept rising higher in the man's face, mottling it reddish purple; the way he kept squeezing the chair arms like he was thinking of ripping them off; the way his voice got louder and sharper.

"You bitch," he growled eventually, sweeping a muscled arm across her desk, making all her precisely arranged possessions rain to the floor. "You absolute bitch. Do you know what it's like? Do you have any idea what it's like?"

He didn't finish but she knew what he was saying. That by being childless, she couldn't possibly understand his hardships. How dare she add to them by banishing his son from school?

"I could just . . ." He mashed a meaty fist into the palm of his other hand, glaring at her with burning hatred.

He didn't hit her, didn't even touch her, but the venom in his voice, in his eyes, struck her like a whip.

Security barged in almost immediately, summoned by her secretary who'd heard the noise. The man was led away. She declined to press charges, because she was fine, wasn't she? Unharmed. But she'd never forgotten the episode. And though she never crossed paths with the man again and heard the family moved away shortly after, she thought she caught glimpses of him in crowds for years afterward, never failing to make her shudder.

But Terry? She'd never imagined anything like this from Terry. And now she couldn't leave his side somehow. Trapped by exhaustion, fear, curiosity.

Jasper brought her some strong black tea with lots of sugar.

"My nan used to say it's good for absolutely everything," he told her with a smile, placing the cup on a small table next to her.

Martha took a sip gratefully. She had been so very thirsty, but the burning hot, too-sweet liquid did nothing for it.

"Doing okay?" Jasper asked gently, kneeling beside her so that his six-and-a-half-foot frame didn't tower over her. He had the most extraordinary eyes, two different colors with golden specs in each. His accent was a melodious mishmash of South African and Chicago's South Side.

Martha nodded, chewing her lip.

"Can I get you anything?" he proceeded, smiling softly. There was a scar bisecting his face, an ugly but healed-over thing, a souvenir from a past life. He was a well-known basketball player once who got "big money crazy" as Ronan, who knew all about such temptations, referred to it.

On the island, Jasper got a chance for reinvention, retraining under Natalie. There was a rapport between the two that Martha suspected went beyond professional, but there was no proof. No fire, only traces of smoke. Nothing in their actions or words, but something about the silences between them.

"I'm okay," Martha replied, forcing a smile. Now that she'd been asked, she realized there was indeed something she wanted. More than that, something she needed rather desperately. Only she couldn't for the life of her place a finger on what that might be.

She'd sit with it, this nameless craving, the way she did with everything else, studying it, trying to figure it out.

Jasper smelled good, she realized. What was that? Sandalwood? It pierced the ambient sterile scent of the room, reaching her with its smooth, warm notes. She leaned into it reflexively, before catching herself and straightening out. What was she doing? What would he think of her? No fool like an old fool. And Martha was all too aware that she was likely one of the oldest people on the island. You couldn't build a thriving community on pensioners and geriatrics. Cruel but true. You had to be practical.

There was Fletcher, of course, but he and Ronan had a connection that went back years, decades even. Some sort of research neither of them talked much about. Fletcher was likely older than Martha, but he was thin, ramrod straight, and oddly powerful for a man who presumably spent most of his life in one lab or another.

"He doesn't look like much of a scientist," Martha had once shared with Ronan.

"What does he look like then?" Ronan had replied, amused.

"Oh, I don't know. A movie cowboy, perhaps, albeit with a penchant for perfectly pressed dress shirts and creased suit trousers."

Ronan laughed heartily. "I'll have you know that Ed Fletcher is the finest scientific mind I've ever come across," he had stated.

"Well, you know what they say about appearances." She looked away, regretting saying anything.

Ronan stepped around to face her. "You're not wrong about the cowboy thing entirely, though. Ed's from Montana, originally. I'm pretty sure if not for his 167 IQ, he'd be rounding up horses somewhere."

One hundred sixty-seven seemed high. Way above average. Martha admitted she was impressed. Perhaps even a bit jealous.

"What sort of scientist is he?" she asked cautiously. Ed's file had come to her heavily redacted. It practically screamed "government work" and "secrets" in narrow, black-ink boxes.

"The best kind." Ronan beamed excitedly. "Whatever he puts his mind to. The man is a genius. A real bona fide genius. You'll see."

Sure enough, over the years, Ed's inventions and ideas had contributed to improving the island dramatically, anything from solar grids to their water desalination plant.

He was seldom seen out, preferring his own company or Ronan's. Whenever he did make it out of his house on the far side of the island, not too far from Ronan's hideaway, Ed Fletcher cut a striking, easily recognizable figure with his starched button-downs and his shock of perfectly white hair.

A nice enough man, but he always seemed distant, even if he was sitting next to you and having a conversation. And perhaps he was—who knew? He rarely talked much about himself or what he was working on. His contributions to their community spoke for themselves.

There were so many times Martha wanted to know more, to find out what Ronan and Fletcher were working on, but she never asked. Boundaries were of paramount importance, and it only worked if everyone respected them. She figured some day she would find out. The island had a way of making one feel like they had all the time in the world.

Martha straightened out, leaning away from Jasper, reaching for the unpalatable tea.

"Have you ever seen anything like that?" She gestured vaguely toward Terry, pulling the focus away from her.

Jasper put his hand on the back of his neck, rotating his head left to right with a sharp crack. "My brother, Thomas, he used to sleepwalk," he said. "When he was younger. I was just a kid. Once, I woke him up. I didn't mean to, I simply didn't realize he was asleep. I got up for a midnight snack." He laughed. "I was a chubby kid if you can believe it. And my brother was there in the kitchen. Just standing there in front of the sink. I started talking to him, asking him if he wanted a slice of the cake too. When he didn't reply, I shook him by the shoulder. And he just flipped out on me. I had never seen anything like it. I started screaming, woke our parents up. They came and pulled him off of me. I had bruises on me for a week in the exact shape of his fingerprints. I was afraid of Thomas too, after that. Didn't want to be, but I was."

"Was he prone to violence? Your brother?"

"Thomas? Violence? No. Never. He wanted to be a veterinarian, was forever rescuing strays and bringing them home, much to our mother's dismay."

Martha looked at Terry, thinking about the story. Because if she wasn't doing that, she'd be looking at Jasper and thinking about what it was she really wanted from him, the thing that wasn't tea.

"So what happened?" she asked finally. "With your brother?"

"He stopped sleepwalking." Jasper lifted his hand palm out as if to say who knew how these things worked. "One day he just stopped."

"Did he become a veterinarian like he wanted?"

"He would have," Jasper replied, with a distant look in his eyes. "But he decided to be a patriot instead and go fight in a meaningless war for his new country."

Martha didn't need to ask any more. Jasper's expression and tone told her all she needed to know.

He was quiet for a moment as if lost in a memory, then blinked, refocusing on the present. On Martha. "Hey," he told her, "you're going to be just fine. So will Terry. Don't fret. Sometimes things just happen. For all we know about the human brain, it is still a mysterious place."

It reminded her of how Ronan talked about outer space.

She smiled to thank the younger man for his kindness, but then her stomach churned. A violent lurch of hunger as voracious as any she had ever felt. Hunger and thirst both, a potent combination, enough to send her reeling off the chair and into Jasper's arms. Her teacup crashed to the floor.

"Hey, hey," he said softly. "I think you better lie down."

But she was already lost to her inexplicable desires, to her all-consuming appetite, to the overwhelming scent of sandalwood and something more primal, meatier, bloodier.

With a groan of pure and violent need, Martha buried her face in Jasper's neck, tearing at the soft flesh there, ravenously chewing her way through the skin and sinew to get to what she craved the most. The relief it brought was indescribable. She wished it would never end.

CHAPTER 15.
JACOB.

PEOPLE WERE LIFTING HIM. Such strong arms. Were they tying him up? What was happening? Jacob tried to talk to them, but his mouth was a desert, its aridness allowing for no words. No sounds but groans.

He could hear everything, though. See everything. In those maddeningly flickering frames his reality came in to view now. Every face held fear but one.

Ronan Bard. There. That expression. What was that? Jacob couldn't find the words.

Surprise? Disappointment?

The possibility of the latter stung. Jacob hadn't disappointed anyone in such a long time. Not even himself. It was one of his favorite things about his life on the island: to look at himself in the mirror every morning with clear eyes and a steady heart and know that he'd done his best the day before and will endeavor to do so again today. He never realized how much he needed that.

Sure, some repairs took longer than he anticipated, and some things were too far gone to be fixed, but overall, it had all been so easy.

And Ronan was the last person he would ever want to disappoint. Ronan, who was closer in age to an older brother, but in significance, a father figure. Ronan, who gave him a chance at a new life.

"What happened?" he heard Ronan ask.

There came a rush of explanations or rather a recollection of the events, for no one seemed to have a proper explanation for this. Jacob didn't either. He no longer felt present inside his body; he'd distanced himself, becoming an observer. It was as if he was watching a movie—a strange and bloody one, not at all the kind he liked—and realizing he was the main character. Or maybe it was like walking into a movie set and confusing it for real life.

Either way, this man covered in blood, with his hands bound, and his words smothered by untold appetites, couldn't have been him.

The only problem was Jacob didn't know how to fix this. For the first time, he found himself looking at a thing broken into parts and having no idea how to put it back together.

There were no tools in his kit, no skills in his back pocket, no adhesive strong enough to repair a broken life.

He wanted to explain this to everyone, especially Ronan. He thought Ronan might understand. Maybe even offer a solution.

But most of all, Jacob Gurley wanted to eat and drink until he was finally full—if such a thing was even possible anymore.

Then he was being walked somewhere, his hands tied behind his back. His feet followed the direction unwillingly, clumsily. Strong hands of others were on his elbows, supporting him, guiding him. A good thing, too, for he could hardly see. The sun was blinding him. Had it always been so zealously bright?

The frames of his movie life flipped by. He was in a room.

White walls. He was tied to a chair. Hushed voices outside. He couldn't see anyone. A sole window offered a view of a tree and the perfectly cloudless blue sky above. It didn't look real.

His first apartment was a tiny basement efficiency with no windows. The rent was cheap because nothing was up to code. He wasn't even sure if it was a legal dwelling or merely his landlord's creative idea of generating extra income. An aspiring artist he was seeing at the time drew him a window on the wall above his bed. It wasn't very good as far as murals went—the dimensions were all off, the perspective was wonky, and the colors were on the acid trip side of realistic—but waking up to a shabbily rendered beach vista beat opening his eyes to the gray nothingness of the wall.

That relationship had lasted less than his lease—only as long as Jacob could fake calm composure and keep his anxieties out of sight. When it came time for him to move out, the landlord declared the wall damaged and kept most of Jacob's security deposit. He didn't fight it. Leaving that place, he knew that the wall was fine, and the real damage lay within him.

This, he knew, was another trick of the eye. Another mural on the wall. Only much more expertly done.

He tried edging his chair toward it, but he was tied to it, legs and arms, which made most movement prohibitive. Eventually, he managed a rocking motion, but all it did was tip him onto the floor.

The thud made the people come back in. The chair was righted with him in it. There was a sting in his forearm, no more than a pinprick. Jacob swerved his head to see the needle retracting.

"What was that?" he tried to ask. It didn't sound coherent even to his ears.

The woman's face was a blur, but a kindly one. She looked familiar but his brain just couldn't make the connection. She said something to him. It was like having words mouthed to him underwater. He felt heavier. She must have given him some kind of sedative. Perhaps he could sleep now and wake up into a more palatable, more reasonable reality.

Jacob had always felt that "it was all a dream" was the cheapest of all narrative tricks but now he would do anything for it to be his life.

Suddenly, he was being moved. Blurred faces all around him. And he was horizontal. They were binding him to the bed. A sheet was pulled over him almost all the way to the chin, making him feel like a child. Someone drew a curtain over the mural on the wall, dimming the light. They were doing everything to make him feel comfortable. Everything but feeding him.

Under the sheet, he tried pulling up his lead-heavy arm, testing the restraint. It held.

Jacob was tired, so tired, but not at all sleepy.

The people left, their voices receding, the door closing behind them.

He flexed his arm and pulled again. And again. And again.

He didn't know how much time passed when the restraint snapped, freeing his arm. His wrist was a purple, mottled mess, a bloody bruise. He flexed his fingers. How clumsy they felt. So unlike the nimble digits that could fix anything, big or small. His fingernails were rimmed in dried blood.

Slowly, Jacob pulled the freed arm across his body to undo the binding on the other side. Then, pushing off the bed, he sat up and took a look around. They left him no food, but there was water on a side table. If only he could reach it.

More struggle with the bindings. A different person must have tied up his legs. Jacob broke a nail trying to undo the knots. He peeled the entire thing right off its nail bed and stared at it. What a strange thing. Nails. Why did anyone need them?

A finger looked more natural without it, just a smooth bloody tip. Jacob pulled on another nail experimentally. It came off with a dizzying ease.

Nails shouldn't do that. The thought came to him through the thick haze of his mind. Perhaps he had surpassed the limits of "shouldn't" now. Perhaps there was a brand-new set of rules for a brand-new sort of man somewhere. Was he evolving? Is this what it felt like?

One by one Jacob pulled off his fingernails, discarding the blackened pieces to the floor like sunflower seed shells.

His hands felt different now. Remade. He untied his legs and swung them over the edge of the bed, slowly lowering them, testing to make sure they could take his weight. Pins and needles erupted everywhere. His body had been asleep, but it was waking up now.

First things first, he staggered over to grab the glass of water from the table. Drinking it tasted like pouring sawdust down his gullet. What was wrong with the water in this place?

Next, Jacob walked toward the mural on the wall. He wanted to touch it, to find out what made it so lifelike. The curtain came off in his hand when he tried to slide it to the side. Such a flimsy thing.

The mural was there, but less bright now, as if reflecting the sun's journey to the west. What a clever trick. Jacob put his hand on it, admiring the bloody perfection of his new and improved fingers. His hand went straight through. There was a crunching sound and small clear shards stuck in his arm. More blood, fresh blood mixing with the old, dried mess didn't mind it that much. It was all a movie, all special effects.

The world awaited him on the other side of this tricky mural thing. The world ought to have something to sate this hunger. Jacob began dragging his body over the windowsill. There was more crunching noise and a sensation of something ripping and tearing, but he didn't stop.

He was emerging from one place into another, a birth in a sense, as violent and bloody as births tended to be.

He hit the ground with a solid thump. The grass was moist, and he buried his face in it, licking it, drinking it in. It tasted better than the sawdust water from earlier, but it still wasn't right.

Jacob got to his feet. He'd never been a particularly large man, but he felt enormous now as if he'd been made into Godzilla by his ordeal. The sun reflected off the glass shards stuck in his body. Shiny. He was glowing. He was magnificent. There was no fear, no anxiety. He couldn't believe he had ever felt either. There was nothing but appetite now. A simple driver, a simple route. All he had to do was move his feet until he found what he was looking for.

"Oh my God," someone said so distinctly that even his muffled hearing conveyed every word.

He couldn't make out their face but thought the blurred oval of it looked shocked. Perhaps it was awe. Awe seemed more appropriate.

The person was backing away from him. Was it so they could see him better? He felt ten feet tall. As huge and as heavy as a statue.

"Wait," he wanted to tell them. "There's something I need."

He had only just been born into this world, and he required sustenance. Could this person not see that?

Jacob reached for them, and they screamed. The sound pierced his ear drums. "Silence," he growled. Then time sped up again.

BEAUTIFUL, ONCE

Only a few flip frames later, and Jacob was feeding. The nourishment was just what he wanted, sating both his thirst and hunger. Juicy, delicious, perfect.

He looked around for the person, to share his feast, but they must have left. Oh well, more for him. He dug in, moaning with pleasure.

There was shouting behind him, distant but coming closer. He should eat faster, he thought. What was this his arm was stuck in? He rummaged around, producing something like a long loop of sausage. Good enough, he'd take it with him.

Jacob tried to get up but fell over. The ground beneath him was slick with dark liquid. He ran his palm over it, then licked it. Strong, salty, metallic. He wasn't sure if it was coming from him or his meal. He tried getting up again.

Something pushed him. A stick? He crashed to the ground, the impact of it jarring him from head to toe. There were people there. Hitting him. He couldn't think of why. Were they mad that he broke their mural?

"I'll fix it," he tried telling them. "Just let me eat, and I'll fix it."

They weren't listening, so he tried batting them away, using his glass-studded arm as a weapon.

There was more screaming. Then a sound came like a sharp clap but louder, so much louder.

He was falling now. In the movie version of this, it took place in slow motion. He could feel his weight shift according to gravity's inexorable pull before slamming into the ground as hard as if he'd intended to go straight through.

The last thought Jacob Gurley had was about all these strange, loud noises that had punctuated his day. Like movie clapperboards, beginning and ending a scene.

CHAPTER 16.
MARTHA.

THE LAST TIME she had a birthday party, she was ten. Her father insisted, telling her how much fun it would be, but even back then Martha struggled to subscribe to his ebullient brand of optimism. Sure enough, no one came. Except for Stanley, the weird, moonfaced, butterfly-collecting son of the neighbors her mother had been friendly with. The two of them sat in the overdecorated backyard staring at each other, waiting out the awkwardness. Martha's mother was already on her first cocktail of the afternoon, and her father had retreated into the house to give the kids a chance to socialize. But Martha wanted nothing to do with Stanley, and he didn't seem to want anything to do with her.

"Why do you collect butterflies?" she asked finally, just to be polite.

"I like the way it feels when the pins go through their bodies," he replied. And just like that, she was done with him, with her party, with the entire stupid day.

Martha went into her room, locked the door, and wrote in her journal for a bit, with tears smudging the ink.

She didn't emerge until late at night when she snuck into the kitchen and ate her birthday cake, with a spoon, by herself. When sugar and chocolate and all that over-the-top, store-bought deliciousness flooded her senses, she was, for the first time since that afternoon, able to stop thinking about the pin-stuck butterflies. She stopped thinking about anything really. There was only cake.

Throughout the years that followed, Martha had tried various diets before eventually resigning to her unfashionably sturdy build, but she had never indulged like that.

Not until now.

Martha Geller dropped the body of Jasper to the floor—what was left of it anyway. Through the sheer somatic pleasure suffusing her veins and the majestic joy of being properly sated, she felt twitches of distress. Eventually, they came into the foreground; the flashing red lights of alarm.

With bloodied hands, she pushed off her chair, kneeling beside the younger man, studying the damage. Had she done this? How could she have? She'd never been particularly strong. How could she possibly be responsible for the ruin of the body before her? The man looked as if he'd been mauled by jungle predators.

Something was wrong. Terribly wrong. Had she been poisoned? What did one do in the case of poisoning? She considered throwing up, but her body roiled in protest, determined to hold on to its terrible sustenance.

Martha got up and walked to the window. Only when she leaned her head against the wooden frame and took in the beautiful, sunny day outside did it occur to her how easily she could move now. Getting down to the floor and getting up had been effortless; she'd done it as smoothly as a child, no knees popping, no groans of effort. She lifted her arms over her head in a tentative stretch, leaving bloody handprints on the wall. Fantastic. All that flexibility.

She slipped outside the room as lithe as a cat.

There. A bathroom. The face that greeted Martha in the mirror looked all too familiar—a broad, heavy square with solid, even features and wrinkles around the corners of her eyes and mouth. An unremarkable face by anyone's account. A serious face. A face covered in blood and viscera.

She gasped, rubbing at it with her hands, only making it worse. It was in her hair too, the reddish tint of henna offset by the russet tones of blood.

Martha turned on the water and scrubbed her hands until their skin felt thin and raw. The water ran down the drain red, then pink, then, finally, clear. She worked on her face next.

There wasn't much to do about the hair but pull it back.

Reflexively, she checked her pocket. The matchbook was still there. A souvenir from her long-dead father. The only sentimental indulgence Martha possessed. Then she brushed a wet hand across her hair to smooth it.

There, all better. Order restored. She was herself now—not whoever she'd been with Jasper, lost to a nameless hunger.

People did that, surely. Lost themselves, lost their heads. So long as they found their way back, all things could be worked out.

She scanned her mind for protocols, but there was nothing there for this particular contingency. Ronan had always believed—naïvely so,

"Crime is a result of social discontent," he'd always said. "We eliminate that here."

"But Ronan," she had protested before, "that's so—"

"What?" He grinned charmingly, raising his eyebrows.

She searched for the right word. "Utopic?"

"But isn't it the point?" he said, eye contact and all. "Isn't that what we're trying to build? A utopia?"

In the early days, there were times when Martha Geller could not believe that she, of all people, a staid and pragmatic person through and through had managed to hitch her proverbial wagon to the likes of an idealist like Ronan Bard. It almost felt surreal when she stepped back to consider it. But being with Ronan, being near him—his words, his conviction, his personal magnetism—had seduced her, erasing all doubt. And Martha, who'd never been a dreamer, had let herself fall for another man's dream. Hook, line, and sinker.

Because this wide-eyed idealism didn't come naturally to Martha, she had relied on Ronan all these years to keep her in steady supply of it. Just as he had relied on her to ground his dreams in practicality, to give them the structure of expectations and protocols.

He was the one flying the kites and balloons, but Martha held the strings. It was how she had always viewed their relationship, how she made sense of it.

Sure, there were exceptions. When it came to Ed Fletcher, for instance, she was completely hands-off. That was Ronan's thing through and through. Just like his hideaway. Not a secret, just . . . private. Nothing wrong with privacy. It was a treasured commodity in a small community like theirs. A respected one.

It was why no one had made a big deal about their one and only banishment. Why no one had talked about it since. A mistake had been made. As good a judge of character as Ronan was he had slipped up. A one-off. Perfectly understandable.

Martha remembered the man, of course, though she never brought him up. A restless spirit who didn't quite take to their serene environment. Always pushing, always prodding, always questioning. A smart man, that much was clear. Fletcher had recommended him personally. But he simply did not fit in. And though Martha wasn't privy to every single detail of what went wrong between him and Ed and Ronan, she knew enough not to ask.

He left comfortably compensated, with an air-tight NDA muzzle. Ronan might have been a dreamer, but he was practical enough when he needed to be. The wound of the rift had healed by now, and everyone knew better than to pick at the scab.

Perhaps this was the same thing, Martha hoped against hope. A mistake. An error of judgment. A one-off. She'd explain it away, bury it, have Ronan's money pave the grave over smoothly. It would be a loss for the community, of course. Jasper was popular and well-liked. But they'd get someone new, eventually. Wasn't that the point of having that journalist woman come visit? Publicity.

At the back of her mind, there was another voice, a smaller one, tearing apart her flimsy excuses, whispering terrible things.

Martha pursed her lips and furrowed her brow, determined to ignore it. She stepped outside just as she heard the screams.

Her first instinct had been to flee. But that would have been irresponsible, and Martha Geller was nothing if not responsible. Besides, one of the main rules of a successful community was helping one another, and the screams she heard were definitely of a distressed nature.

She didn't realize Natalie had pipes like that on her. The woman had such a quiet speaking voice. She was one of the easier choices Martha and Ronan had ever made, someone seemingly meant for the island. A perfect skill set to mindset ratio.

They both knew the arranged marriage hell the woman had left behind; both were pleased by how well she fit in here, where all the choices were at last her own. She'd even chosen her new name. The island truly was her happy place. But she did not seem happy now, standing over the ruined body of the man who had been her assistant and perhaps much more than that.

"Natalie," Martha began in her most authoritative and calming voice. Her school principal voice. "Natalie, please."

The woman turned around. Her darker skin was blanched white with shock, matching her coat. The scream died on her lips as she faced Martha, then began to re-form as her eyes scanned the older woman.

Why? Martha wondered. And then she realized that although she had washed her hands and face, she did nothing about her clothes.

"Stop screaming," Martha said firmly. And when the woman failed to comply, she lunged at her with the speed and strength she didn't know she had, pushing Natalie into the wall, clamping a hand over her mouth.

"Stop screaming," Martha repeated, trying to sound reasonable. "There's been a terrible—"

Natalie bit her. She'd never been bitten before. The sheer surprise of it made Martha pull her hand back. The scream hit her anew, but there were words to it this time.

"What did you do? What the hell did you do?"

"I did Hell's work," Martha almost replied. "Don't you see?"

She'd never been a believer, and being Jewish, she certainly didn't grow up with the traditional Biblical idea of Hell, but now, having done what she'd done . . . Martha Geller was willing to consider alternatives.

Worse yet, she suspected it wasn't over. The small voice in the back of her mind was getting louder, and Natalie's proximity felt irresistible.

Martha was hungry again. A great roiling sensation, like a wave reappearing on recently becalmed waters. But she couldn't. . . She couldn't . . .

Natalie tried to fight her off, but Martha was larger and stronger now too. She used her own hands for shackles as she locked them around the younger woman's arms, pushing her firmly against the wall.

The screaming Martha could almost ignore. The warm, mint tea-scented breath on her face, the spittle. The hunger—she didn't think she could.

A single indiscretion was understandable, a sole mistake forgivable. But not a repeated one. Martha knew better. She had decades and decades of rigid discipline to fall back on. It had always given her life shape and structure, but it had corseted her in a way, too. And now she felt like it was crushing her ribs, suffocating her.

All these rules. A life full of them. And yet nothing in it had ever felt as good as the thing she had just done, the thing she was considering doing again.

Once you realized your needs, once you'd succumbed to them and began contemplating a repeat performance, the Rubicon had been crossed.

"Do it," said the voice inside her. "You know you want to."

Suddenly, Martha felt light as air, as if a simple push was enough to send her in any one direction. As if there were no rules, merely desires. And nothing felt more tempting than to give in to them.

Martha leaned toward the young woman, stopping her mouth with her own. She'd never much cared for bodies, of any gender, but this was a kiss unlike any she'd experienced. She found a snaking tongue and bit it off. It tasted divine. Two bodies entwined, locked in what appeared to be a hungry passion but was in fact a passionate hunger. Martha proceeded to devour the woman. Soft, supple, all for her. No more restraint. No more shock, no more horror of her actions, of her unfathomable appetites. Only freedom. Only pleasure. It was even better than an unshared birthday cake.

CHAPTER 17.
ARDEN.

THIS WAS WHAT *war journalists must feel like,* she thought, staring at the macabre scene before her. Personally, Arden had never understood the appeal of extreme reporting. She liked a good story but the farthest she was willing to go for it was . . . well, a beautiful, nicely appointed island. She'd never be able to report from the front lines, with bullets whizzing by, and the smell of death in the air. She didn't even like roller coasters.

Secretly, she suspected that her unwillingness to go to extremes was the reason her career had by and large stalled. They were all living in a sensationalized age of heightened drama and rampant emotions. To succeed, you had to be willing to give the people what they wanted. And what they wanted, more often than not, was blood—real and metaphorical.

Arden's brand of investigative journalism was more along the lines of letter openers used to slice at the envelopes to free their secrets, not blades used to slash at flesh to see how it bleeds. She wasn't "knives out" enough and knew it. Forever the girl made fun of at sleepovers for crying during scary movies.

Which made processing what she was seeing now so much harder.

The wrecked bodies. The blood-covered man lying beneath the bell. What was that?

"What is this?" she asked Ronan, unable to keep the tremble out of her voice.

There was an annoyance in his expression as he turned to her, but brief, blink-and-you-miss-it. Had he not realized she was following him? Certainly, this wasn't something he would want an outsider to see.

"Arden, would you kindly go back to the house or guest house and wait for me?" he said, his face neutral now, his tone perfectly even. "I'm afraid this is something of an internal matter."

She thought of a million retorts, anything from sarcasm to recrimination, but what good would it do? The truth was, she was curious, yes. She knew there was suddenly way more of a story here than she had anticipated. So much more than the golden boy genius' utopia that initially met the eye. But she also knew with equal certitude that there was something profoundly wrong here on the island. Something that went deeper than seeing dead bodies in this ersatz town square. Something evil.

And Arden wanted to be away from it, as far as possible.

"I should stay," she told herself. "I'll make my career on this. It's an opportunity of a lifetime." There was a part of her that wanted this—to push, to get up close and personal, to find the ugly truth, to set all fear aside and excel. To stop settling for a middling career and the mediocre life that came with it: her dull boyfriend, her plain apartment, her last year's clothes. "Stay and find out what else is there," her better angels sang in unison.

But then she saw the mangled lifeless bodies—*the bite marks on them*—and she ran.

It would objectively be difficult to get lost in a place that small, but shock tended to have strange side effects. Arden had been so sure she was moving toward Ronan's house, but she somehow found herself in the woods. Out here, the bucolic scenery was a whiplash to what she had just witnessed, the grotesque scene that had seared itself into her retina.

Arden stopped and sat down on the ground. It was more of a collapse. Her legs had simply given up on her, having carried her thus far. Her mind was still racing a mile a minute, but her body was exhausted.

She looked around. All these trees, she didn't know the names of them. Were they native to the region? Did Ronan terraform this place to suit his needs? Had she been more knowledgeable about nature, perhaps she could guess this place's location. Ronan's people took measures, ensuring she had no clue where she was going on the trip over. She joked with them to cover her discomfort, telling her it made her feel like being in a spy movie. And the island's location, for her as for everyone other than the islanders, remained a mystery.

Perhaps Chris was right to worry, she thought. Would she ever get back to the mainland to tell him that? He certainly loved hearing such things. Most men did, didn't they?

Maybe not Ronan. Arden could not figure him out. One moment he'd be warm, present, considerate, his attention like a beam of sunshine. The next, he seemed distant, aloof, a dreamer caught between two worlds.

Good looking, smart, personable: Ronan Bard could have done

anything with his life. This was the thing he chose to do. She didn't know whether to admire or question his choice.

What would she write about him? How would she describe him? What words would convey the feeling of being with Ronan, his peculiar balance of hopefulness and sadness? He hid the latter, but she could see it, lingering behind his eyes. Though she did not possess the courage of some, Arden prided herself on being able to read people well. And Ronan, to her, read like a man who'd had his heart broken. She just wasn't sure of the details.

Live long enough, hard enough—put yourself out there and reach for the stars—and the world will break your heart as sure as night follows day. Ronan did better in that respect than most, but something had to have happened. Something to make him refer to the years out of the spotlight and before the island as his happiest.

Arden wished she had gotten more out of him. She wondered if she would have the chance to now, then chastised herself for such callousness. People were dead. People had been killed. People who were alive and happy only this morning, a mere few hours earlier, going about their business, enjoying their paradise.

It was ruined now, this place. It would never be the same. Never free of this.

There was a rustling up ahead. Arden sprung to her feet, her heart pounding. What was that? An animal? She was never particularly outdoorsy. She'd once broken up with a guy over a proposed hiking trip, realizing she would never be serious about someone who could casually enjoy themselves without a proper toilet.

A tall man came through the woods, squinting at her with what could have been amusement or disdain. He was older, well into his sixties if she had to guess, but his shoulders were broad, unbowed by age, and his hair was a wild mess of pure white.

"Did I hear the bell?" he asked.

"Y-yes," she stammered a reply.

"Why?" He raised a bushy eyebrow at her, and she noted that, unlike his hair, it was black.

"There was a—" Arden started crying. It was as if someone had reached inside her and turned on a faucet. She seldom cried and never in front of random strangers. It had to be shock. From now on, all aberrant behavior could be ascribed to shock.

It wasn't just tears either. These were loud, heavy, gulping cries. An unburdening of a sort, gutting in its potency. The weight of it pushed her back down to the ground.

The man shuffled from foot to foot, looking distinctly uncomfortable.

"You must be the reporter," he said finally.

For some reason that worked better than any "there, there."

"I am," she said, looking up, wiping her eyes.

'So." The man clapped his hands together. "Report."

There was something about his manner that told her this wasn't a man who spent a lot of time with others. On purpose.

Arden got back to her feet. The man was too tall. From the ground level, he seemed like a giant. He wore a neatly pressed, white button-down shirt with its sleeves rolled up to his elbows and a pair of chinos. Not exactly hiking attire, but people on the island tended to wear exactly what they wanted, with "do what thou will" serving as the main fashion motto. She'd seen a man wearing Superman pajamas at the café, looking perfectly at ease.

Arden wiped her eyes again, then pushed her hair back with tear-wetted fingers, composing herself.

"There's been a murder," she said. "Several murders. It happened down by the bell."

The man said nothing, just stood and stared at her.

"Who are you?" Arden asked. The question came out without being thought through. What was a man his age doing on the island? Sure, he looked strong, but wasn't the idea to have a younger population, people who could contribute physical labor? Was he someone's father? Ronan's was dead, she knew. Martha's? No, he didn't look old enough.

"Is Ronan there?" he said, ignoring her question.

"Yes."

"But you are not," the man observed, almost as if to himself.

"Ronan asked me to leave."

"And you came here?"

"I got lost."

He sighed heavily, and Arden thought what a sight she must seem to him. Disheveled, weeping, helpless like some clichéd damsel in distress. She had played into the stereotype before, strategically, to get help, attention, a story. But she had never felt like one until now, and didn't much care for it.

She brushed the dirt off her jeans and looked up at the man trying to project confidence she did not feel.

"Aren't you going to ask me more about the murders?"

He tilted his head to the side, bird-like, studying her with open curiosity.

It was so quiet in the woods, so serene. Words like murder did not belong here. *She* did not belong here. Yet the old man seemed perfectly at ease. Calm. Too calm. Arden would have suspected him senile, but he looked too sharp, too knowing.

Without bothering to reply, he turned away from her and began walking, presumably heading back to where he came from.

"Come with me," he tossed over his shoulder.

"If I want to live?" she quipped, cringing immediately, annoyed that her penchant for movie quotes in times of discomfort was choosing to showcase itself now of all times.

"Oh, no," the old man said, without turning around. "I'm afraid it is much too late for that."

CHAPTER 18.
MARTHA.

A LOUD SOUND startled her, though she wasn't sleeping, merely resting after a perfectly satisfying meal. Was it a gunshot? Martha had always felt about guns the way most people felt about snakes: while in theory, she knew they were harmless when inert, in action, they were much too deadly not to fear.

Back on the mainland, a sound like that more often than not turned out to be a car backfiring, but here . . .

She got up off the floor, studiously avoiding the ruined female form crumpled there. What good would it do to dwell on this? It was done. Martha took a deep, steadying breath. She would just have to find a way to move on.

As she cleaned herself up in the bathroom once more, Martha thought to look in on Terry. Was he still unconscious or did the noise wake him up? It was certainly the day for it. The loudest of all. A most unusual day in every respect.

But she was still herself, wasn't she? She didn't buy into the "you are what you eat" thing for a second. Nor did she think a single deed, or two, had the power to define an entire life. She waited until the water ran clear before shutting it off. This time she actually thought of changing clothes, but even if Natalie had a spare outfit on the premises it would have been much too small for Martha. She would just have to make do with what she had on until she had the chance to go home and change.

But first Terry.

The baker was lying in bed, supine, peaceful looking. Should she trust his sedation? Martha reached out tentatively, touching his shoulder. His eyes sprung open. There was nothing of Terry in their darkness.

Martha pulled up a chair just outside of his reach, to sit by the foot of his bed and contemplate the man as he thrashed against his restraints, angry moans and spittle flying from his mouth in lieu of words.

What would Ronan do? she wondered. For all his kindness, he could be mercurial in times of adversity. Besides, he likely had enough on his plate today, with the journalist and everything.

And wasn't it Martha's purpose, the one she had so gladly accepted and relished, to make Ronan's life easier?

She never thought of it as living in Ronan's shadow; it was more like basking in his sunshine. A perfectly comfortable state. There were so many ways to feel comfortable, to be comforted. It was something she could offer him in return—the sweet bliss of ignorance.

It didn't take long to find and collect flammable liquids. The place proved accommodating to her needs. The loss of equipment would be lamentable but recoverable.

Martha had turned it round and round in her head like a puzzle, and this was the only thing that made sense. Clean the slate, start over. There was another thing, an unacknowledged desire in the back of her mind. She *wanted* this gone. Wanted to wake up from this strange nightmare to nothing but a pile of ashes.

Martha spared Terry one more glance and shuddered beneath his unblinking dark stare. Then she left the building, carrying a bottle of liquid with her, a homemade Molotov cocktail, with a piece of fabric for a stopper.

She lit it outside, using the book of matches in her pocket. After all this time, they had come in handy. She thought of her father smoking his Camels as she struck a match. It took a single try, obsolescence be damned. The fabric caught on fire, and Martha lobbed the bottle inside the white building marked with the ancient Rod of Asclepius. It sailed through the air like a strange comet with its fiery tail. More sounds, and then nothing but flames, the warmth of them like the sun.

Martha watched their dance, mesmerized. Then she turned around and walked away.

Though never a fan of aimless ambulation, today she let her feet carry her, feeling like an observer of her own body's actions. Away from populated places—smart. But where to? Home?

She realized her destination only once she was nearly there. Janice Mann's place. Of course. Martha could feel the magnetic pull of it like a migrating bird.

She had always liked Janice. In her own way, she even admired the woman. Though they were nearly the same age and had both had their share of disappointments on the mainland, Janice had the sort of strength that Martha did not. It had nothing to do with rules or discipline and more with an innate steeliness of character and sturdiness of purpose.

Where Martha had chosen to orbit a star, Janice had always charted her own course. The woman was formidable. A powerhouse content to exist as a lighthouse, proudly alone, with only her work and her dog for company.

Martha wasn't sure she could do the same after all these years spent at Ronan's side. Back on the mainland, she wore her solitude like a hair shirt, but here she had found ways to mitigate it. And, reluctantly, even learned to enjoy it.

In principle, though, she admired the self-containment with which Janice carried herself. They could have been friends in another life; perhaps, if only they could break through some of their carefully built walls. But friendships were complicated. It was better to admire from afar.

Martha saw Jupi before he saw her.

She'd never been much of a dog person, but Jupi had won her over ever since Ronan first got him. There was a purity about the ball of fur that touched her. Purity was rare; she had seldom been around it, even back in her old life. She spent her time dealing with kids, but they had always seemed too jaded by the world by the time they came to her school.

"I could get you your own," Ronan said, smiling at her with the puppy.

"Oh, no." She shook her head. Deep down, Martha suspected she didn't have the reserves of kindness or the ability to sustain what kindness she did have, and that was surely required for taking care of another being.

She visited Jupi throughout the years, bringing him treats. She even got used to that ridiculous name.

"Why would you call him that?" she asked Janice originally.

"Because." The woman held up her hand as if revealing something obvious. "Jupiter, the planet. The gas giant."

"Uh-huh."

"Well." Janice laughed, rolling her eyes. "You should see this dog fart."

She did—see it, smell it, joke about it. Of course, it changed nothing. The dog grew up to be smart, devoted, purpose-driven, much like the woman who raised him.

"Jupi," Martha said to him now, raising her voice a bit. "Come here, boy."

The dog saw her, gave a wag of a tail, and ran toward her. He stopped a few feet short of her outstretched arm, suddenly uncertain.

"Come here, boy," she repeated.

He growled lightly and backed away. What was that? Did he forget her? She looked down at her ruined clothes. Was it the blood and viscera staining them?

She squatted down to the ground to get closer to his level but also to obscure as much of her ruined outfit as she could.

"Where is Janice?" she asked him, looking around.

Jupi was intelligent enough to roam around on his own, and the place wasn't large enough for him to get lost, but he usually never strayed too far from his person.

From this distance, Martha could smell the dog. It surprised her. The dog with his superior olfactory faculties could surely smell her, but vice versa? Jupi's smell was good, earthy and meaty and . . . edible? No, that wasn't right. She shook her head, forcibly dislodging the thought.

Jupi growled louder this time, then turned around and proceeded to move away from her. Martha got up to her feet. How strangely easy it was now, as if someone had lubricated the decades off her joints.

The dog turned his head as if inviting her to follow. She did, keeping her distance.

They came to the clearing where Janice's house stood. The woman liked a bit of privacy, though not as much as some. Certainly not as much as Fletcher.

The front yard was strewn with wood and woodworking projects in various states of completion. Martha ran her hand across one of them, admiring the live edge finish.

"Janice," she said, announcing her presence. "Janice, it's Martha Geller."

The introduction was unnecessary, but she enjoyed a formality here and there, a hint of structure to a conversation.

There was no reply. Martha approached the house, peering through the living room window. It looked the same as always, like the inside of a fairy tale log cabin. Its owner wasn't inside.

She must be in her lab, Martha thought. Probably studying the space ball from this morning. Was it only this morning? It felt like it happened a week ago. What a day this had been.

Her stomach made a sound so loud that she crossed her arms over reflexively even though there was no one around to hear. Was she really hungry? Again? How was that possible?

Martha put her hand on the side of the house to steady herself through a wave of dizziness. The wind came, blowing her hair in her face. It smelled like fire, she noted, and other things she did not want to think about.

Jupi watched her with a baleful eye from a safe distance. She tried smiling at the dog but couldn't be sure if her face just then could be made into a smile.

It was quiet out here—too quiet, like her ears had suddenly popped, taking with it all the sound. Martha cautiously proceeded to the lab.

It was a generous name for it, she had always thought. An

aspirational one. The place was decently equipped but with a pronounced homegrown vibe to it. A hobby den. Ronan was always encouraging this sort of thing, but Martha, who made sure the bills got paid, knew the difference between a part-time pursuit and a passion project. She'd seen on occasion the state-of-the-art equipment Ronan ordered for Fletcher and himself.

Janice's lab was a small building, no more than ten by ten, and the outside walls were decorated with a mural of a periodic table, artless but meticulous.

Martha knocked, then pushed the door. It was unlocked, so she announced herself once more and took a step across the threshold.

The light poured in from the large window that took up the top half of the wall opposite the door. The table in front of it spanned from wall to wall and was covered in a myriad of things Martha wasn't sure she could name. Gadgets and doodads as her mother, forever scornful of technology, might have said.

The center of the table was cleared and given to a single object—the space ball. It was glowing softly in the ambient light, making Martha think of a strange, round eye.

She realized then how desperately she wanted to touch it. To lay her hands on it and feel its warmth, for she was sure it was warm. Would she? Should she? The table around it appeared blackened as if charred, though there was no way of telling whether this was from the space object or something else before it. Still, it made it look menacing—a darkly rimmed eye like that of a wrathful pharaoh.

Martha paused, her arm outstretched. She took her first step toward it as if in a dream. Outside, Jupi barked. The dog was usually the strong, silent type. The barking had a sharp note to it, every so often descending into a mournful bellow.

The spell broken, Martha went to check on him. Seeing her, he ran behind the house and disappeared. She followed.

When Martha rounded the corner, she stopped and stared. The tears began streaming down her face, stinging the tender, washed-raw skin. She couldn't remember the last time she cried, didn't think she knew how to anymore. It all felt distant from her—the horrific tableau behind the house and the wetness on her cheeks as if her face had sprung a leak.

What if none of this was real? What if she was still back in a white room, unconscious, recovering from Terry's attack? Wouldn't that make so much more sense?

And if none of this was real, if she was merely having a terrible nightmare, then what did it matter what she did? Why not take a step forward and then another? Why not kneel before the dead body of one of the few people she had ever admired? Why not reach out to test if it was still warm?

It was. Unsettlingly so. Hot like fire. Or perhaps the fire was in Martha's hands. She had been overheating all day, dismissing it as hot flashes typical for someone her age.

Murder. Martha had never seen the aftermath of a murder. The body was laid out carefully amid the too-tall grass, unseeing eyes to the skies. The murder weapon was right there, next to Janice's left hand. A scalpel. The scientist in Janice might have appreciated the gesture.

There were cuts all over Janice's body. The largest one Martha could see across the woman's neck—a red, jagged smile, its edges raw, glaring skyward like a hungry mouth.

Martha shuddered. *Janice wouldn't appreciate this* she thought. The woman was all about precision. This was sloppy as if done by a shaking hand. A hand belonging to a body at war with itself.

Martha dared herself to look closer. The other cuts were much the same. Ugly slashes betraying rage or uncertainty or something else altogether. There was so much blood that the grass around Janice had changed color; the green mixing with red to produce a distinctly unpleasant shade of brown.

There were bite marks on the woman's forearm. They looked alarmingly human.

The sound came back suddenly. Martha could hear Jupi crying at a distance. The poor thing must have seen this happen. She wanted to comfort him but was sharply aware that she had no comfort to give. She was different now, blood fed and fire forged. She had, she realized curiously, become someone to fear.

The smell of blood and torn flesh made her swoon. Her stomach gave a nasty lurch. Without thinking, she reached down, pulled out some brown grass, and stuck it in her mouth. It tasted good but bitter. Nothing like Jasper. Nothing like Natalie.

Martha shuddered again but continued chewing the grass. Experimentally, she prodded Janice's torn wrist with her finger. A piece of flesh came off—or had she just pulled it off?—and found its way into her mouth. Same as the grass: good, but bitter. She took another, horrified of herself yet unable to stop. What was she becoming?

Discipline, she told herself. *Get a hold of yourself.*

She closed her eyes and balled her hands into fists so tight that she could feel her fingernails digging crescent moon slivers into her palms. There, now count. One, two, three. Breathe. Breathe. In and out. In and out.

A vision came to her, a knowledge unveiling itself—a scene playing as clearly as if someone had turned the backs of her eyelids into a projection screen. When she opened her eyes, she knew with dead certainty what happened to Janice Mann. Martha saw the woman's last moments alive. More than that, she *felt* them in her bones.

Janice coming out of the lab, backlit by the menacing glow of the object behind her, a terrible new appetite suffusing her veins. Janice barely resisting the urge to make a meal of her beloved dog companion. Janice biting her own arm to stop herself. Janice, all too aware of something being terribly wrong, staggering around her property. Janice feeling herself turn into something *other* but unwilling to let herself become transformed.

Janice Mann, forever stronger than Martha, taking her own life. Her body screaming in protestation, self-preservation halting her hand. One jagged cut after another. Determined, terrified, desperate. Alone.

Weren't they all alone out here once you took away the illusion of community?

Janice smiling at Jupi, telling him she loved him, shooing him away. Janice bleeding out into the grass, her life force returning to the earth, her eyes on the sky that had sent such an unfathomable, horrible gift.

Martha collapsed on the ground next to Janice. She felt all her strength leaving. Everything that made sense, everything that made her Martha Geller, was disappearing.

When she was hollowed out at last, the darkness flooded in.

Some time later, Martha got up and returned to the lab. She took the object from the table, the weight of it heavy but manageable. She felt strong, purposeful. A woman with a task.

She tried different ways of holding it, eventually settling on putting it behind her neck and supporting it with her arms, feeling like Atlas carrying the weight of the world on his shoulders.

BEAUTIFUL, ONCE

Hers was smaller of course, but the world never needed to be large. Just look at this island, such a perfect size.

Martha blinked away the sweat out of her eyes and slowly, steadily began walking toward the main street. She'd ring the bell and gather them around in the park. After all, she had something wondrous to show them.

CHAPTER 19.
ARDEN.

THE WHITE-HAIRED MAN didn't seem like the type to talk and walk. Arden followed him silently through the woods, questions popping in her mind like popcorn.

Her thought processes were bifurcating, then splitting further; the tributaries carrying them miles away from the origin source.

Part of her was here on the island, present and alert, desperate to find out what was happening if only to make sense of this increasingly surreal day. Another part, trembling with fear, was rewinding time, going back to her safe, uneventful life, her plain, cozy apartment, the familiar comfort of her boyfriend's arms.

There was something else too. Another part, a much smaller one, slowly emerging from some deep, dark recesses of her brain, burning its way to the surface. It felt angry—the anger that comes on the heels of fear and helplessness. There it was, scratching at her insides like hunger.

Arden pushed it down and away.

They came upon a clearing. The older man stopped, harrumphing loudly. Arden stopped too, a few feet away from him.

She brushed her hand against the back of her neck; the collar of her shirt was soaked with sweat.

"Home, sweet home," he said. Was that sarcasm?

Arden looked around. There was a lot to take in, but out of the several structures on the property, one immediately pulled focus. It had a large round base with what looked like a curved top made of reflective panels that split open to reveal unfathomably intricate machinery.

It looked vaguely familiar. "Is that—?"

"An extremely large telescope?" he finished her sentence dryly. "Why yes, it is." The man took in her expression with some amusement. "Come along now."

"I'm not stupid, you know," she bristled reflexively at his back as they began walking again. "I can understand scientific concepts without having them dumbed down for me."

He stopped, turned, and arched an eyebrow at her. "Well, then, perhaps you've heard that telescope builders are a remarkably unimaginative bunch when it comes to naming their creations, hence gems like Very Large Telescope in Atacama or Large Binocular Telescope in Arizona. Extremely Large Telescope was indeed the chosen name for the latest, greatest darling of the European Southern Observatory, destined once again for the Atacama desert. Only they'd run into one too many budgetary snafus and . . ." The man snapped his fingers, making the sound like dried twigs snapped in half. "Et voilà! The project scrambled. Sold off as scrap to the highest bidder."

"Ronan," Arden exhaled, impressed despite herself.

"Ah, yes." The man smiled tightly. "Ronan does like his toys."

It did look like a toy, she thought, all shiny silver and slick surfaces. Like a giant transformer robot.

"Does it work?"

"Of course, it works." The man scoffed. "It works all too well."

Arden picked at the enigmatic remark as they continued their walk. She hoped the man would explain himself in time.

There was a house near the telescope and another one farther away: plain, solid structures, though the distant one appeared to have been made mostly of reflective glass. The white-haired man led her to the closer one. It had a no-nonsense bunker feel to it.

"I don't enjoy house guests," he said, pausing at the door.

"You want me to stay outside?" Arden asked, failing to keep the snark out of her voice.

He chewed his lip, studying her face. He seemed on the brink of saying something, then changing his mind. Instead, he opened the door and ushered her in.

It was bunker-like on the inside too; rather, a cross between a bunker and a well-equipped laboratory. Nothing homey about it, she observed, though perhaps there were rooms in the back appropriated for living spaces.

The man led her to the nearest corner of the space where on the cleared edge of one of the tables, there was an electric kettle, some mugs, and a box of Twinings Darjeeling tea.

Gesturing her to sit down in one of the wheeled desk chairs, he set about getting the water from a conveniently located industrial sink and prepared it to boil.

Arden felt like Alice in Wonderland, lost in a strange place, seated in a chair too large for her frame.

"What's your name?" she asked to kill the silence. "Who are you?"

"Ah." He lifted his long index finger. "The questions begin. You know, I would have advised Ronan against bringing you here."

"Why didn't you?" she shot back. Hostility bred hostility, though she'd keep it tea civilized.

"We've had a falling out recently," the man said, taking a seat in another chair that perfectly fit his height. He used his feet to roll closer to her.

They studied each other for a moment. *He looks fiercely intelligent,* Arden thought, wondering what he might see in her.

"My name is Edward Fletcher," he said finally. "I don't like handshakes."

"My name is Arden Raleigh. I won't offer one."

His lips quirked in mild amusement. "How are you enjoying our island paradise, Arden Raleigh?"

"I was enjoying it very much until I saw the dead bodies by the bell."

She felt like they were in some absurdist play. Worse yet, like she was in the audience, struggling to follow the plot, and someone pulled her out and thrust her onto the stage, telling her to wing it.

Fletcher rested his elbows on the chair's arms and steepled his fingers under his unevenly shaved chin.

"You must forgive me, Arden," he said after a while. "It's been a very long time since I entertained. Do you like tea?"

"Sure. Unless you have anything stronger."

He got up to shut off the kettle and poured the steaming water into two mismatched mugs, throwing a tea bag into each one.

"I have a feeling it'll be best to keep our wits about us," he said, handing her one of the mugs. It had an anthropomorphized former planet Pluto cartoon on it, looking devastated with a thought bubble that read "How could you?"

"Cute," she commented.

"Isn't it just?" He smiled. "I find it matches the décor."

She looked around the spartan, personality-free surroundings pointedly.

"Thematically," he clarified.

"Ah."

The tea was hot and strong. The first sip singed her taste buds, but it was good to feel something, anything, other than confusion and fear.

Edward Fletcher sipped his tea like his mouth was made of the same metal as his equipment. The steam fogged up his glasses. He took them off, shook them, and put them back on.

A strange man, Arden thought, *but not a silent one*. She just had to find a way to get him to talk.

"How do you know Ronan?"

Fletcher took a deep breath and let it out slowly. "Ronan and I go way back," he said.

"To the time before the island?"

The man nodded.

"Before the apps?"

He shook his head.

Okay, good. That gave her a timeline. So Fletcher was a part of Ronan's infamous lost years.

"Did you come here with him? Were you one of the original settlers?"

The wording felt off to her, as if she was discussing a British colony and not a rather recent, in the grand scheme of things, social experiment.

"Oh, no," the man said, looking away. The steam got to his eyeglass lenses again, making his expression unreadable. "Ronan and I had parted ways by then. We didn't reconnect until later. He invited me to come, and I accepted."

"You seem to have a lot of falling outs," she pointed out, venturing onto thin ice.

Fletcher seemed amused by that. "We have our share. It's unavoidable, I'm afraid. We're too similar in some respects, too different in others."

"Are you related?"

He laughed softly. "No, no. Only in spirit."

"What do you seem to fall out about the most?"

The man shook his head. "Life," he responded nebulously.

"That's very vague."

"No, it isn't." He fixed his cuffed sleeve. "It's simply a rather large umbrella for very specific subjects."

"Okay, sure," she replied, playing along. "So what's your take on life?"

Edward Fletcher took a sip of tea, considering his answer. "By and large," he said slowly, "I consider it wasted on the living."

His words sent shivers down her spine. She took a sip of tea to chase them down.

"You mean, the way youth is proverbially wasted on the young?"

He lifted the corner of his mouth momentarily. "Mm. Quite."

"What are the alternatives?"

He sat down his cup and ran his fingers through his hair. It did nothing to tame the wild disarray of it.

"Have you ever watched the news and then switched the channel to a nature documentary?"

"Sure," Arden said. She must have done this at some point, some restless evening alone, channel flipping.

"And did you ever spare a thought to how much more harmonious, more beautiful it would be if the world had just been left to the animals?"

"Humans are animals," she countered.

He wrinkled his nose in dismay, his glasses moving up and down. "Once, perhaps. But they have since devolved."

"You mean evolved?"

He narrowed his eyes. "No, I do not."

It dawned on her then. The nature of Fletcher and Ronan's conflicts. One man disdained humanity, the other tried to save it. One believed Earth would be a paradise without people, the other built a paradise for the select few. And yet they were here, together, butting heads or not. The yin and yang of morality, keeping each other in check.

"Ronan disagrees with you," she pointed out.

Fletcher sighed. "Ronan is a complicated man."

"That's diplomatic."

"It's true," the older man asserted.

"I don't doubt it." She shifted gears. Sometimes it created a whiplash in an interview, sometimes it gave it momentum. "What does the telescope do?"

He smiled, proudly, proprietarily. Like a collector asked to talk about his favorite artifact.

"A hundred thirty foot diameter segmented primary mirror and a fourteen foot diameter secondary one. Adaptive optics. Six laser star units. Autocorrection for atmospheric distortion and images approximately ten times sharper than most existing telescopes can produce."

"What is that when it's at home?"

Fletcher smiled and sipped his tea.

Patronize me, Arden thought, *I don't care. Just tell me what I need to know. Make me understand all this.*

"It means the telescope outside has approximately two

hundred fifty times the light gathering area of Hubble and can produce images up to sixteen times sharper."

"So, what, prettier pictures?" She played dumb for levity.

He laughed. "Exactly right."

"But seriously? What do you do with it out here in the middle of nowhere?"

Fletcher tapped his index finger to his chin. "We do the same thing everyone has been doing since the beginning of time, Arden. We look up to the stars and wonder if we are alone."

CHAPTER 20.
MARTHA.

SHE COULDN'T DECIDE if she had been walking for a very long time or no time at all. But she knew the place she was coming to now was different from the one she left earlier that day.

The screaming, the crying, the rushing around. It was madness. Chaos. Martha hated it.

All this time spent making sure their small world ran as smoothly as a well-oiled engine and now this?

No. No, it wouldn't do.

Martha made her way to the bell, carving her path like a knife through the raving mob. She found with some alarm that she could not recognize any individual faces. She knew these people like the back of her hand; every one of them had entered her life as a collection of data that had once passed through her desk, and later became acquaintances—almost friends, neighbors.

Now she could not make out who they were. All the faces blurred together. It had to be the rage twisting their features, the blood covering their skin.

Where was Ronan? Where was he when they needed him most?

She would just have to do it herself. After all, over the years she'd become accustomed to doing the heavy lifting.

In this instance, it was literal. As Martha approached the bell, she sat the glowing sphere down. There was blood on the ground all around it, she noticed idly. Blood seemed to be everywhere lately. Once it had seeped into the ground, what terrible harvests would they sow?

She couldn't feel her hands; they were all pins and needles. It was probably the blood flowing out of them from having them raised all that time while carrying the object.

With numb fingers, Martha reached for the clapper and began ringing the bell. The sound of it was deafening.

Ronan had acquired it on a whim once. A two-to-one scale replica of a bell from a famous shipwreck uncovered in the waters not too far from the island.

"It'll give the square some character," he declared, as excited as a young boy with a new toy.

Personally, she didn't think it boded well for the island, but she was reluctant to give voice to it, thinking her sentiment would be dismissed as superstitious, or, worse yet, inane.

Besides, she liked Ronan's enthusiasm: the way his face lit up when he brought new things to the island, always improving it, always trying to make it better for everyone. Approving his actions was her way of feeling selfless by proxy.

She didn't need to be good, only good to him, which seemed infinitely more manageable. And over time, she learned to be a better person. It was so much easier out here.

"Do you know how in the suburbs everyone says hi to one another and in the city no one ever does?" he'd asked her once, a long time ago, back when most of this was still merely a dream.

Martha nodded, thinking how she avoided all manner of interaction with strangers no matter where she was. Not even eye contact if she could help it.

"Do you ever think about why that is?"

She recognized the question as rhetorical and let him go on.

"It's about the numbers. Fewer people make it easier to appreciate them, to greet them, to wish them a nice day or happy holidays. In the city, there are simply too many people to do that. Happiness, politeness, decency . . . it all gets watered down. You cannot sustain it en masse. Never."

She nodded along some more. He'd used this in his speeches and interviews since. Always driving home his point of "small is good." Talking of the future belonging to micro-communities. Predicting the collapse of larger nations. Speaking of building a better, kinder world. Or living better, kinder, more meaningful lives.

Martha didn't disagree with any of it. She simply didn't have his heart or his faith. It boiled down to the fact that she simply could not bring herself to care enough. But she believed in Ronan, and that was enough.

Her opinions, she found, were malleable to an extent. The Martha Geller who woke up this morning was a better person than the one she left behind on the mainland.

The Martha Geller of the present moment—well, the jury was still out. She couldn't quite get a hold_of herself long enough to form a judgment. Events and thoughts kept moving, shifting. How many terrible acts did it take to turn a good person bad? When did one stop being able to forgive the sins and still love the sinner?

Who was she now?

"A monster," a small voice whispered in the back of her mind with relish. "You are a beautiful monster."

She shuddered. And then felt the heat of the praise ignite her. Because wasn't it praise? The voice had certainly made it sound like one.

Ronan had always been generous with praise too, lavishing her with it, never taking her for granted. Where was Ronan now? Martha could not find him in the sea of blurred faces before her.

She'd save them all, even if he couldn't. This thing she brought them . . . surely, it was enough to atone for all her sins.

She continued ringing the bell until it was all she could hear. Until it was the only sound in the world.

And then she saw them, gather around as she had hoped they would. Some came willingly, some looked as if they'd been forced by others. It was difficult to tell.

What was in their faces? Pleasure? Anger? Rapture?

Martha let go of the bell's clapper. There was no need for the clamor anymore. All eyes were on the object now, and, as if sensing it, the orb glowed brighter and brighter. It was like looking directly into the sun and knowing that the sun was looking back.

An incomparable moment of perfect connection.

And then it exploded. A sound like the universe ending. A sphere breaking itself apart into a million shards, each finding a home within the flesh of the people surrounding it.

Martha, who had never gotten a tattoo or a piercing, who had never even understood the appeal of such things and sometimes silently judged those who did, felt the shards entering her skin and welcomed them. She imagined them traveling through her: epidermis, dermis, hypodermis, layer after layer, slipping into her bloodstream, sailing down her veins like tiny metal ships, straight into her heart. The object was a part of her now—its message her message. She had always excelled at being someone's right hand.

No longer purely herself and now never alone, Martha moaned her satisfaction, forgoing words. The people around her echoed her sentiment.

What were they now? Hosts. Accepting others into the inner sanctum of their bodies. Sharing is caring, wasn't that the rule? Like good hosts, they had to feed their guests.

The hunger swam to the foreground now, potent enough to obliterate all else. In a voice that sounded like hers mixed with another's, perhaps the one from the back of her mind, Martha bellowed a rallying cry. Then she fell upon the nearest warm body and began to feed. The shard-studded crowd around her followed suit.

Afterward, time lost meaning. There was no time at all, no more minutes and hours. Only before and after, only desperate hunger and sated satisfaction. Only those who moved and those who didn't.

Somewhere in the distance, the sun was setting, igniting the sky. Or perhaps it was fire, crawling closer. Her face caked with gore, Martha could smell nothing but blood.

Was it fire? How could you tell when you carried the flames inside you? Each embedded shard like a glowing ember beneath her skin.

Maybe it *was* fire inching closer, and maybe that was a good thing. Clean the slate and start over. Didn't they do that with forests? She would just have to find Ronan and figure it out. They did it once. They could do it again.

As soon as she felt strong enough to get up, she'd look for him. Right now, she just needed a bit of rest. It had been such an eventful day.

Martha scanned the faces around her. She couldn't make out

their features but thought they looked happy. Good, she thought. I made them happy. Ronan would be proud.

Then she thought she spotted him at a distance. He was carefully coming closer. She didn't need to see his face, she'd recognize him anywhere. Ronan Bard: the beautiful, ageless Peter Pan, the hopeless romantic, the last dreamer.

Before she knew it, he stood next to her, over her. His face as bright as the sun.

"Look," she wanted to tell him. "Look at all I've done for you. It was a mess, but I cleaned it up. Just let me get up, and we can go. We can start over."

But her innards felt glued together, from her stomach to her mouth, and no words came. Martha tried to convey her meaning with her eyes, but there was blood in them.

She could hardly see, but she thought he was looking at her strangely. Was he not impressed? Was he not grateful?

"Ronan," she cried, and it came out as a growl. "Ronan, please."

"Oh, Martha," he said at last. There was a quiet devastation in his voice. "Oh, Martha."

He extended his hand toward her, and she thought, yes, he finally understood her, he was helping her up. She reached to meet it and heard a sharp loud sound. A car backfiring, she thought. Why was there a car?

Her body was thrown back sharply, the shards inside her protesting.

Martha hit her head on the ground hard, and all she could see was unbearable brightness. She imagined it was Ronan's face, but it might have been the sun.

No more loud noises, she knew. Only this. Pure light, pure heat. Her eyelids seemed as heavy as velvet curtains. Martha felt them pulling toward each other—the end of the show, the brightness reducing itself gradually to nothing but a distant star. And then she closed her eyes and there were no more thoughts and no more stars. Only silent darkness.

CHAPTER 21.
INTERLUDE.

A MAN WALKED across the land he had come to know like the back of his hand, thinking how foreign it felt to him now. He had dreamed of space exploration for so long, and now it was as if he had found himself on a distant planet, navigating its strange terrain, fighting its unfamiliar gravity, and wishing for nothing more than to be back home.

The sun had baked the blood on his skin into a thin crisp like the top layer of crème brûlée He didn't know how much of the blood was his. He'd tried to be careful, but it was impossible to avoid all of it.

The sweat was pouring down his face, and he had to keep wiping it off with his forearm. He was on fire but felt the shard of ice inside him stubbornly refuse to melt.

Shock, it was shock. He'd regulate after calming down and regrouping. After all, it wasn't that hot of a day. Sunny but moderate, with low humidity. A beautiful day by all accounts—or it would have been if not for everything that had happened.

He tried considering it logically, step by step, the way he had always done when dealing with problems but it was impossible.

Thoughts slipped through his fingers like water, like sand. They jumbled together, refusing to line up.

Images came to him like violent flashes. Grotesque visions. Nightmares.

It didn't fit; none of it went with what he knew life to be. He desperately wished he was dreaming, but that was merely a cheap storybook trope. In reality, you did not wake up into a better world. You built a better world and hoped it stuck around to wake up into, day in and day out. But not like this. Never like this.

There were things he knew he should be feeling—sadness, devastation, fear, guilt, shame—but there was only numbness inside him, a terrible absence. A void.

He'd never been good with emotions, but over the years he had learned them like an actor learning his lines. He got good at it. It was easy enough; the only trick was putting thought where others were guided by feelings.

He had always structured his relationships accordingly, allowing for a proper distance, a small sense of mystery.

There were only a few times when he allowed himself more freedom. It did not go well. But in retrospect, it was, at least, interesting.

"I'm not breaking your heart," the only woman he'd ever loved told him a long time ago. "I don't think you have one."

Brutal at the time, but what a valuable lesson.

He rebuilt his walls, taller than ever. Chose other passions to pursue. There was always something to explore for an insatiably curious mind. The world was full of wonders. And when you ran out of those, all you had to do was look up.

As far back as he remembered, he had always wanted more. The restlessness drove him on like a whip in a merciless hand. Here on the island, for a while, he had found something like peace. It felt magical. At first.

It was like taking the hourglass of time, laying it onto its side, and enjoying how much it looked like an infinity symbol. Or perhaps it was like breaking the hourglass altogether and sticking your feet in its spilled sand.

Metaphors fell apart. Words betrayed. Opinions got misunderstood. But actions spoke for themselves. He would explain himself through actions, he decided, as he set about making a difference. It was so easy here on the island, where the world was small enough to lull you into believing it could be anything you wanted it to be.

The man stumbled, and failing to break his fall with his hands, tumbled down. Getting to his knees, he looked for what tripped him. A leg.

He tentatively nudged it with his foot. It rolled. The leg had no owner. It didn't belong to some beachgoer playfully buried in the sand to trip up a passerby. There was only the leg with its mottled flesh and a bit of bone sticking out.

He'd retch, maybe even throw up, but his body felt completely empty, like he hadn't eaten in days.

The man looked around, only then realizing that he was on a small beach, one of the few on the island. And then he saw it. A pile of limbs. A small tower of them. It made him think of pyramids and altars. Offerings and sacrifices.

Someone had done this. Reduced people to bodies, bodies to shreds. It seemed unfathomable, even after all he'd seen. And here, on this serene beach, with the azure waves gently lapping at the golden sand, it was grotesquely out of place.

Some of the sand wasn't golden anymore, he noticed. It had been marred by blood.

If he had gasoline and a match, he would set the limbs on fire, turning them into a pyre, something meaningful, something reverent.

There was already a smell of fire in the air. It would be befitting.

Instead, he picked up the leg and brought it to the pile, placing it there, like a missing Jenga log.

He used his left hand. The right one was occupied. He didn't dare look at it.

His left hand was shaking. The limb fell and rolled, and he had to pick it up and place it on the pile again. The sand beneath his feet was reddish brown, too wet for being so far away from the water.

He backed out of it, backed away. The bodies smelled like death. Of course they did. He turned away and caught the scent of fire in the wind again. Sharp, acrid: It would have made him gag had it been closer.

He thought of going to find the source of it, but somehow it didn't seem to matter anymore. It felt too late. Besides, there was only one place he wanted to go to now. If his feet would carry him. It felt impossibly far at the moment.

The ocean looked tempting. Perhaps the water would soothe the flames dancing beneath his skin. He took a few steps toward it, but then a thought stopped him. It seemed irrational, but what if the sea would extinguish him, like a candle? What if this strange fire was his life force now, the inferno he'd tried to keep at bay for so long manifesting at last?

The man stopped and watched the waves rolling in. Once upon a time, that alone could soothe him. Now, he could find no solace here.

Releasing a deep sigh of sadness, he turned and resumed his walk.

His feet felt leaden, unwieldy. As if the pull of the Earth had been thrown into overdrive or broken. There was a tingling pins and needles sensation in his fingers and toes—like he had slept funny and was only now waking up.

Not unpleasant, just peculiar.

He thought about his destination and what he'd do once he got there. He would have liked to form a plan, but nothing stuck. He'd play it by ear, wing it. It had worked for him before.

One notion jabbed at him persistently: What if he arrived and no one was there? What then? He had relied on few things in this life, and fewer people, but he couldn't bear the thought of finding himself alone.

What would that make him amid all the dead? A grave keeper in a paradise turned cemetery?

He shuddered. Wiped the sweat off his brow.

How nice it would feel to lie down and close his eyes. What he wouldn't do . . .

No, he told himself firmly. He had a goal, a mission. Without these things, he was nothing. With them, he was infinite. He could fix this. He could fix everything. With a lever long enough and a fulcrum to place it upon, he could move the world.

The man stumbled on, the weight on his shoulders crushing him worse than any gravity, for nothing was heavier than broken dreams.

CHAPTER 22.
ARDEN.

"**D**O YOU THINK we are?" she asked. "Alone?"

The white-haired man took off his glasses, rubbed his eyes, then began to laugh. Quietly at first, then louder, as if he'd been told a joke and he alone knew just how funny it was. Unsure what to do, Arden waited.

She thought of Ronan and all the clever, preprepared questions she didn't get to ask him. They were all written down in the app on her phone and in a notebook she carried in her pocket. The former was by and large useless here and likely didn't have enough charge. The latter made her feel like a real journalist. What she'd wanted to ask was:

With the perspective of time, would you revise any of the statements you made earlier?

Have you reconsidered any of your politics? Especially, your stance on immigration.

Your critics have referred to this place as Neverland. Do you ever think of it as such?

What do you see as the future of the island?

Did any of it matter now?

"You're thinking about Ronan," Fletcher said, his laughter finally dying down.

"I am," she confessed.

"He does that." The man nodded. "He gets into your head."

"Is he in yours?"

Edward Fletcher crossed his arms, tapping his left elbow with the fingers of the right hand. "I suppose I've come to enjoy his contradictions, infuriating as they may be."

"He seems fairly straightforward to me," Arden offered, though it wasn't really the truth, simply something to keep the conversation going. "A man who dreamed a dream and had enough money to make it a reality."

"You know what's always fascinated me about dreams?" the older man said. "How quickly they can turn into nightmares."

A smile died on her lips.

"Does Ronan feel the same way?" she asked.

Fletcher unfolded his arms, pulling at his shirt sleeves. "Ronan is the smartest person I know," he stated. Then added with a smirk, "Besides myself, that is."

"Is that your answer then? That Ronan is smart enough to see every angle?"

"Oh, no." Fletcher shook his head. "Not *every* angle. That wouldn't do at all. Just think how boring that would be."

"Boring?" The word rubbed her the wrong way. "We're talking about people's lives."

The man studied her for a while with something like amusement or perhaps pity. "Oh, I get it," he said quietly after a while. "You think all of this is real."

In high school, Arden had a friend who claimed her dreams were more vivid than reality. So much so that she struggled to tell the difference. Arden didn't believe her, which eventually led to the dissolution of their friendship. In retrospect, she'd since realized that it wasn't distrust but fear that pushed her away. A fear that things might not be as she believed them to be, that the boundaries between worlds might be more malleable than she was comfortable with.

"Is it terrible?" she remembered asking her friend then—curiosity-driven even as a teenager.

"Oh, no," her friend replied. "It's kind of like magic." And Arden felt a sharp stab of jealousy because there was nothing magical about her own life.

Long after their falling out, her friend slit her wrists in the bathtub. The right way: lengthwise. And Arden never got to know why, but deep down she had always suspected that it had something to do with her dreams. Because once the magic stopped, what else was there?

"Isn't it real?" she asked the older man now. "It seems real enough."

"It's a game played by a child who's had every toy in the world," Fletcher said simply.

"Like Peter Pan in Neverland?" she supplied, remembering her notes.

"Don't worry. You're not Wendy," he quipped.

No, of course, she thought. *Martha would be Wendy. Only she stayed.*

"And you are Hook?"

He laughed a full-bodied laugh at that. "You're very amusing," he told her. "But no, Hook was but a minor distraction. I would be the ultimate villain of the story."

"And who is Pan's ultimate villain?"

Fletcher tilted his head back as if forgetting that there was nothing above them but a ceiling. Then he brought it down slowly, fixing Arden with an intent gaze. "Time," he said. "No greater villain than time."

She thought of what Fletcher's life must be like, out here all by himself. All this science and not enough human interaction—how that could warp a mind.

"Are *you* bored out here?" she asked, picking up an earlier thread.

He shrugged. "I have my work. My experiments."

"But why are you on the island if you don't think any of this is real?" she pushed.

"The telescope is here."

"That's it?"

He rubbed his chin. She waited, idly noticing how long his fingers were, how large the knuckles.

"I've run into some trouble back home," he told her at last. "And no, before you ask, it was nothing prurient, nothing salacious. I didn't sleep with undergrads or embezzle research funds or whatever your reporter's mind might concoct."

She smiled. "So what then?"

"Oh." Fletcher waved his hand dismissively. "Ethics or some such nonsense. Everyone wants to know the truth but is too smothered by political correctness and societal norms to actually do anything about it."

I bet there is a story there, she thought. Then said it out loud.

"But you didn't come here for me. You came for Ronan."

"I didn't know about you," she joked lightly.

He shrugged, unamused. "Ronan would have stolen the show, even if you did."

"Do you hate him?"

"Hate him? No." Fletcher seemed taken aback by her question. "I love him like the son I never knew I wanted sometimes."

"Really?" His sense of humor left her discombobulated.

"More like a protégé," he said, correcting himself upon reflection. "He was so bright. So curious. So . . . full of surprises."

"Was?"

The white-haired man sighed deeply and shifted in his chair. "Do you know the very worst thing for a smart person?" he asked her.

It felt like a quiz, and he acted as the stern, demanding professor.

Arden fell back on levity to hide her discomfort. "A lobotomy?"

Fletcher smiled indulgently. "Try again."

"Tell me."

He pursed his lips before speaking. "Happiness."

"Really?"

"Oh, yes," Fletcher assured her. "Happiness is pure poison. It stops progress, creativity, drive. Necessity is the mother of invention. Adversity is the father of ingenuity. All happiness has ever bred is laziness."

She chuckled awkwardly. "That's a rather unique way of looking at it, isn't it? People crave happiness above all else. The pursuit of it is literally enshrined into our Constitution."

"If you believed everything you read in old papers, we'd still be living in the Stone Ages," he countered. "Or, at least, stoning ages."

"You don't believe in the system. The same as Ronan."

"Not the same," he asserted.

"How so?"

"I don't believe in any system," Fletcher explained. "Ronan

believes in small, easily governable ones. For my money, gather more than a few people, and it's bound to go to hell."

"Was that what you fell out about?" she asked, seizing the thread. "Or were you simply disappointed that Ronan got happy-dumb out here?"

She felt brazen now, like a proper interviewer, holding back no punches. It was almost enough to make her forget about the bodies in the square. Almost.

Fletcher paused, studying her.

"Are you familiar with the saying about a tree falling in the woods?"

"Sure, yes," Arden replied. "Isn't everyone?"

"Well, if a utopia is built and no one talks about it, is it really there?"

She inclined her head in a touché gesture.

"It's how we differ, you see," he explained. "I'd be perfectly happy with my work out here, on my own. But Ronan wants attention, praise. It was almost charming when he was young, but now it's rather . . ." he chewed his lip before spitting out, "embarrassing."

"It's why I'm here, isn't it?" she asked.

Silence.

"It's why he sent out his golden record," she pushed.

"Ah, yes." That animated Fletcher. "He's like a young boy showing off his shiny toys. But a personal golden record . . ." The man shook his head. "Such hubris."

"He told me he sent it out with a destination in mind."

Fletcher began laughing again. Another unsettlingly timed outburst.

"Did he now?" He got up and started pacing. "I advised against it, you know. I told him not to do it."

"Why not?"

Fletcher stopped and cast his eyes skyward through a small window, one of several in the otherwise bunker-like walls.

"When I look at the night sky, I see darkness," he said quietly. "I do not want it to look back at me, to know me. But Ronan . . . Ronan sees adventure and possibility."

"He wants to believe," she said, paraphrasing an old TV show.

"Oh, no," Fletcher said. "It's so much worse than that. He actually does believe, you see. Ronan Bard thinks he can stretch his utopia all the way to the stars. He can't bear the thought of someone up there not looking or caring. He can't stand the idea of being alone. And so he believes."

"And you don't."

"No," he stated firmly, grimly. "I've seen too much of the world, of the universe, to let myself believe that."

"You make him sound as naïve as a child," Arden observed.

"Not at all. You'd be surprised by how skeptical a dreamer can be. Ronan firmly believes in preparedness. He even—"

Fletcher caught himself, cutting off the sentence abruptly. He clapped his hands loudly, rubbing them together.

"Heck of a story for you, right?" He smiled. "Trust me, you'll get your money's worth here."

"You make it sound like I paid for a ticket to the show."

"But you have, in a way." Fletcher continued smiling as he cracked his knuckles in a staccato rat-tat-tat. "Due to a quirk of timing, you're getting the greatest show on Earth."

"Because of the murders?"

He did not reply.

"Well, look, I don't know if you're following the news from the world at large, but murders are commonplace these days. There's a mass shooting every week or so. There are wars. What happened here is a tragedy, but—"

Edward Fletcher held up his hand. "Let me stop you right there. As charming as your righteous indignation may be." Arden opened her mouth to protest, but he continued speaking. "What you're witnessing here isn't some senseless, garden-variety mass murder you have become accustomed to back on the mainland."

"What is it then?" she asked sharply.

"In case you haven't noticed," he replied, "it's a morality lesson."

The words hung in the air between them heavily, ominously like rain-laden dark clouds. Arden was just about to ask for an explanation, when—

A man burst into the bunker house. Eyes wide, hair a mess, his skin and clothes covered in blood and viscera. He moved steadily, but effortfully, dragging his body along like a deadweight. The door, or perhaps the threshold, threw off his balance but he was righting himself now, moving awkwardly as if he didn't have full control of his limbs. He was virtually unrecognizable.

A war movie extra. Someone from another world. But you could not mistake the object in his right hand for anything other than what it was—a gun.

"Ronan," Edward Fletcher greeted the man with disturbing calmness. "You always knew how to make an entrance."

"Ed."

Ronan stopped moving now. He stood in the middle of the room, lightly swaying on his feet. Sweat was pouring down his face, and he kept mopping it up with his left arm, leaving dirty smears across his face.

"Long time no see," the older man said as if this was a casual visit. "But I knew you'd come today. It's a day for visitors, it seems." He gestured to Arden.

"Always a step ahead." Ronan grimaced as if the words were difficult to get out. "I suppose you saw this coming, didn't you, Ed?"

"I did."

"And you didn't try to warn me? Didn't try to stop it?"

"No," Fletcher said simply. "I did not."

Ronan groaned and fell to his knees, his legs cutting out from under him. He caught himself with his left hand on the floor, never letting go of the gun in his right; yet, he was seemingly not fully aware of it. He looked like a strange caricature of a sprinter about to take off, but also like a man on the verge of collapse.

"Why?" He croaked the question effortfully.

If this was a movie, the director would have used the trick of zooming in on the main two players, cutting out Arden, the side character, and making her disappear into the distance. She felt like a witness to a drama that had begun unfolding long ago and was finally coming to an end.

"I could ask the same of you," Fletcher countered. "I told you not to, but you proceeded. Why?"

Ronan Bard pushed off the floor back into a standing position, the effort screwing up his features into a grotesque visage.

Arden studied his face. Gone were the movie star handsomeness, the easy smile, the carefree charm. Like they were never there to begin with. Like the mask had been ripped away.

Awash in blood, sweat, and tears, Ronan emerged looking like any newborn—small, vulnerable, scared.

He looked around, blinking to clear his vision, his eyes finally alighting on Arden as if seeing her for the first time.

"Not the interview you were hoping for," he said almost sadly. "I apologize."

He moved toward her, and she took a step back involuntarily. Guns made her nervous. The man holding one before her, in his present state, did more than that.

Ronan clocked her reaction and stopped moving. "Any more questions for me?" he asked, but there was no energy behind his words for a mocking tone.

Arden could not speak. The sheer terror of the situation had ossified her curiosity.

He tried and failed to smile, then wiped at his face once more, dragging a bit of viscera from his sleeve to just under his eye. Slowly, he turned to Fletcher.

"Right again, Ed," Ronan told him. "Perhaps inviting a journalist wasn't the best idea."

The older man looked at him patiently, like a teacher acknowledging and accepting his pupil's confession of wrongdoing.

"Why?" Ronan asked him again, a pleading note in his voice.

The man said nothing.

"Okay," Ronan said. "I'll go first. You were right." He cringed, though Arden could not tell if it was from the admission or something else. "All this . . ." He waved his gun hand in the air, making Arden's heart skip a beat. "The island. Everything. All this happiness," he practically spat out the word, "it wasn't enough."

Arden thought of an early song by one of her favorite artists that began with, "I had a dream I got everything I wanted . . ."

"I tried and I tried," Ronan continued, "but it was just so BOOOOORING." He shouted the last word like a tempestuous child, flecks of spittle flying out of his mouth.

It made Arden flinch, but Fletcher only shook his head at him sadly.

"So I sent out some messages," Ronan continued, his tone lower now, almost guttural. "But I never expected this." He used his gun to gesture again, making Arden's stomach plummet.

"Of course, you didn't," Fletcher told him softly, almost kindly. "You were just a boy spitting in the wind."

Ronan looked at him pleadingly.

The expression in Fletcher's eyes hardened. "Well, look what the wind had brought you back," he said, and the words seemed to crush Ronan.

"I never thought it would be like this," he whispered, almost too quiet for Arden to hear. "Why did it go like this?"

He seemed so young now, a boy king to Fletcher's ancient wizard.

"It's like I always told you," the older man said. "It's a dark and scary world out there. You can't have it both ways, locking down *and* reaching out."

Ronan shook his head, then lowered it. "My message was of peace. I wasn't even sure anyone would ever see it, let alone respond."

"You were always much too arrogant for something that simple," Fletcher said. "Besides, I may have changed a few things and course corrected a bit."

When Ronan lifted his head, his face, beneath the dirt, was white as a sheet. He was trembling with anger. Arden had seen him at his best, then at his worst, but she'd never thought of him as ugly before. He was hideous now: rage-contorted features and dead eyes.

He lifted his gun and fired.

The older man crumpled to the ground, a red stain spreading across his white shirt.

This was it, Arden realized, shocked by how calm she was. This was how it all ended. The best story of her life, the worst day of her life. She didn't even know where she was—where this fallen paradise lay.

What a strange and terrible fate.

Ronan turned to her. Their eyes met. She saw fire in his, its flames being slowly extinguished.

"The tech won't work," he said with perfect calmness. "But there is a boat. The other house, my house, has maps, provisions." He took a key out of his pocket, dropped it to the floor, and kicked it over to Arden with his foot. "Go. Find your way back. Tell your story. Tell them—" He searched for it. "Tell them it was beautiful, once."

"What about the island?" she whispered.

She thought she saw tears in his eyes, but she couldn't be sure.

"Let it burn," Ronan replied softly, his voice breaking.

He paused as a violent shiver shook his entire body. He threw his arms around himself like he was trying to prevent coming undone at the seams. "I'm sorry, Arden," he said so sincerely that she almost wanted to tell him she forgave him.

"I'm sorry," he repeated, lowering himself to a sitting position, cradling the gun. He looked like a small boy now, scared and lost. He looked like the Ronan Bard she met earlier, a gracious host, a lovely man.

"Come with me," she told him. The words came out of her mouth without thinking.

"Oh, no," he said with quiet conviction. "I belong here."

With that, Ronan Bard lifted the gun and put it in his mouth.

Arden closed her eyes. She didn't want to see any more death. She granted the man before her one last courtesy of privacy.

The sound of the gunshot reverberated off the bunker walls deafeningly, jarring every bone in her body, throwing her to the floor, causing her to hit her head.

Arden didn't know how much time had passed: a minute or an hour. She only came to her senses and moved when she heard Fletcher groaning. Her vision blurry but focusing, she followed the sound, locating him by the door. With a blood trail behind him, he looked like a comet straight out of a nightmare.

She got up, walked over, and knelt beside him. He was alive but just barely. There was so much blood outside of him that it seemed impossible any was left inside.

"You cannot leave," he said in a ragged whisper. "You've been exposed."

His words made her shiver despite the heat. "Exposed to what?"

"Whatever Ronan's extraterrestrial friends sent us over this morning."

The dots that were only tentatively connecting before began to knit themselves together. The man must have noticed it in her expression.

"Oh, yes. You see, Ronan got his reply, after all." Fletcher tried to laugh but all that came out was blood. "He always got what he wanted."

"And you saw it coming?"

"I did. Quite literally. It really is a very good telescope."

"And you didn't do anything?"

"I did not."

Arden didn't think she had ever hated anyone before, not like this, not like it was the only feeling in the world. Stronger than love, stronger than anything.

"Why?"

"Because," Fletcher croaked, each word a monumental effort, "Ronan was right. It is so boring. You got to make your fun where you can find it. He had his experiments, and I had mine."

"I'm glad he shot you," she told him, infusing it with venom.

"Me too," he said. "I was getting so tired of it all."

His body convulsed violently, making his eyes fly wide open as if faced with an unfathomable and terrifying sight, and then he was still.

In the movies, people usually closed the eyelids of the dead, but Arden did no such thing. She wanted Edward Fletcher to remain forever staring at the last thing that frightened him. Wherever the man was headed, she wanted him to never know peace.

EPILOGUE.

WHEN SHE VENTURED OUTSIDE, her first thought was that the world was on fire. It wasn't here yet, but it was coming. She could smell it. She could see the air shimmer with it. For a moment, Arden was mesmerized by the distortion, by the way it changed the sky into something utterly foreign and strange. An optical illusion. Nothing more than that. She rubbed her eyes to clear her vision.

The smoke was molding the air around her, choking her.

The other house, Ronan said. Yes, she did see another house on the walk over here. How long ago it seemed. Before all the revelations. Before the two men had unraveled the world around her, leaving her alone in what remained.

Arden forced herself not to think about anything but survival. Nothing that had happened, nothing anyone had said—most of all Fletcher's terrible words—mattered now. All she had to do was get away from this place.

She could see the other house now, rippling through the fire curdled air in the distance. She took off her shirt, tied it around her face, and ran toward it.

The door was locked but Arden had the key. She didn't remember picking it up earlier, but she must have. It felt warm as if Ronan had just handed it to her. The lock opened smoothly.

On the inside, the place was nothing like Fletcher's bunker and nothing like Ronan's other home: all high tech but decorated in a way that put Arden in mind of old science fiction with its technicolor, wild imaginings of the future. It was a boy's playroom and a man's command center all at once. A sleekly professional environment with a whimsical soul. It broke her heart a little to think of how much this place reflected the man who built it and would never return to see it again.

She found maps on the bookshelf next to a hardbound collection of Jules Verne. Provisions were in a small makeshift kitchen off to the side. Military-style MREs, water bottles, things in small, clearly labeled pouches. It was strange to think that someone with so much faith in his experiment would have all this. But he also had a gun. Fletcher was right, after all—Ronan was a contradiction.

Arden couldn't even imagine at that moment how she would tell his story. First things first, she had to get off the island. She found a backpack in the corner and began packing. The bag was large, tactical, and by the time it was full, Arden could barely lift it. Knees bent, back angled, she tried again. Survival strength: She needed it then. The sort of thing that made people lift crumbled, impossibly heavy walls off victims during rescue missions.

She straightened out as much as she could, given the weight on her shoulders. The last thing she did was grab the boat keys from an anchor-shaped wall hook.

Outside, it had gotten worse. The fire was coming closer. Arden could hear the loud crackling noise as it began to devour the trees. The smoky smell made its way through her ersatz face mask. She heard another noise too, and it took a moment to place because it sounded too ordinary, not at all like something to be found in a nightmare—a dog barking.

She looked around and saw a large, shaggy mutt. Was she hallucinating?

As a child, Arden was bitten by a neighbor's dog. It left her with an age-faded scar on her right calf and a lifelong mistrust of dogs in her heart. She overrode it only occasionally and effortfully, but if there was ever an occasion worth the effort, it was now.

"Come here, boy," she beckoned, struggling to make herself understood.

He approached her cautiously, stopping a few feet away. Up close, she could see that his snout was graying, though he still seemed youthfully energetic and strong.

"We're leaving," she told him simply and proceeded toward the coast. He followed, keeping a steady distance between them.

Arden knew nothing about boats and was relieved to find that Ronan's was a small one. It looked like it would be simple enough to operate.

It was white with a blue stripe across and a half roof over the center part. Its name was Eden, calligraphically done on the side. No surprise there.

Wading into the water, Arden dropped her backpack into the boat, then waited for the dog. Reluctantly, he crossed the distance between them and jumped in. She untied the rope that kept the boat tethered and followed the dog.

There was a dashboard not unlike what one would see in a car. Arden had driven cars. *Please, please, be as easy as that,* she thought, offering a small prayer to the universe. She inserted the key in the ignition and turned it over. The engine sputtered, then caught. It sounded strong, eager to move.

BEAUTIFUL, ONCE

Arden untied the shirt around her face and put it on. *Eyes front,* she told herself, but then, without meaning to, she looked back at the island. In the shimmering, hazy air, she thought she could see nightmarish shapes emerge back on the land. The dog barked. Could he see them too? Perhaps he was merely telling her to move.

She turned away, spun the wheel, and advanced the throttle. The island, all it was and all it had become, receded into the distance.

Arden had tried to amuse herself by imagining that her life was a movie with her as the lead—a plucky heroine—and her time on the boat as a montage, sped up highlights over a rousing soundtrack.

In reality, it stretched forever, making her lose all sense of temporal presence. She had never been good at reading maps and even once famously got lost in a shopping mall, much to her boyfriend's amusement. Now, on the paper before her, she could see the swathes of land separated by blue water expanses, but she could not figure out how to get to them.

The center roof provided some refuge from the heat, but not enough. The sun beat down on her mercilessly, blistering her skin, piercing it layer by layer, until she felt like she was on fire in and out. From time to time, she'd take her shirt, soak it overboard, and put it back on, but the relief was always short lived. She offered it to the dog once, but he shrugged it off. He didn't trust her—though she saved him, though she fed him—and he continued to stay as far away from her as the boat's confines allowed.

After all he must have seen on the island, Arden supposed she couldn't blame him. He looked sad, and she thought he was probably missing his owner.

The prepackaged meals were flavorless despite what their labels promised. She forced them down her gullet for nutrition, but they left her gagging. The dog didn't seem to mind, though his approach to eating was slow picking at the food throughout the day. There was no way to tell if that made it more palatable or less.

The water Arden knew to ration, especially because it was for two. It was always too warm and never refreshing. She took tiny sips, pouring the dog's share into a small shallow bowl from one of the ready-made meals.

Most of the time Arden wrote. There was a notebook and some pens in Ronan's backpack, and she used them to make sense of her thoughts. When she tried reading them back, a lot of it seemed like a strange cross between fantasy and mad ravings. Some made no sense at all. Then again, what happened didn't either.

Increasingly, the island seemed like a dream. Well, a nightmare. It was so much easier than attempting to explain it all.

She had even tried it as a fairy tale.

Once upon a time, there lived a beautiful prince. He was rich beyond compare and blessed with every good fortune. But he grew weary of his kingdom, for it had belonged to his father and his father before him, and the prince left to build a kingdom of his own.

He found land far away, small and surrounded by the sea. And it was beautiful too. The prince sent word telling those who looked for a new home and a second chance to come and live in his land. They came and helped him build his kingdom, and for a while it was as perfect as the dream that had started it all.

The prince had a right-hand helper by his side who made

all things possible, and a wizard who lived in a castle of his own and taught him things. He had every comfort in the world, and he was beloved.

But one day, the prince got bored. He looked around his new kingdom and realized he wanted more. He looked to the stars above, and shouted his name to them, telling them, "Behold all I have done." But they said nothing back, and after a while, he stopped expecting them to.

Only his wizard continued to wait for a reply. And one day, it came. And it was terrible.

The wizard had warned no one, nor had he told them that he had changed the prince's original message to the stars, for the wizard was an evil one.

What came from the stars was madness and fire and death. It had obliterated the prince's kingdom. Crushed by the weight of the wizard's betrayal, devastated by the destruction of his dream, the prince chose to stay in his ruined kingdom forever.

The end.

Yes, that was good. The story worked so much better as a fairy tale with its grandiose highs and stupendous lows and a moral woven through it all.

Arden read it aloud to the dog, her voice low, parched from thirst. The dog listened, inclining his head, which she took for approval.

There, she mused. *At last, I have written a good story.* Should she stick it into one of the empty plastic bottles and send it out to sea? Would it find an audience? Would they read it and learn?

The next day, delirium set in. There were times when Arden

felt like she never left the island. Like she was back there with Ronan, burning, burning.

She saw things in the water. Strange and terrible things that could not possibly be there.

She had even seen Ronan out there, still alive, swimming after her. "And why not?" her fracturing mind whispered. "You never saw him die."

Once she caught herself wondering what the dog would taste like. Surely, it would be more palatable than the MREs. But no, a maddening thought crossed her mind, *one must never bite the things that bite back.* It made her want to laugh. She could feel unhinged, maniacal laughter bubbling up in the pit of her stomach, and knew if she let it out, she'd never stop.

Arden tried to think of home and Chris, but it all felt impossibly far away, like a past life, like a distant planet.

Every so often, she thought she saw flames dancing on the water. It would have been beautiful if it wasn't so terrifying.

Sometimes the dog's bark would cut through it, and she remembered to take a sip of tepid, plastic-tasting water. Once, she dreamed the Extremely Large Telescope came alive and snared her, its eyes turning into a giant mouth and chewing her, chewing her, piercing her flesh with tiny sharp points and tearing it asunder.

Sometimes in dreams, there was Ronan screaming in her face: "*BOOOOORING!*" Occasionally, he was joined by Fletcher, the older man's shirt soaked red, blood pouring out of his mouth.

Most of the time, Arden wished she could stay awake, but she simply had no energy to do so anymore.

The boat was never meant for a long trip. Perhaps a quick jaunt by a knowledgeable sailor, but never this. Arden poured the last of the water out for the dog and settled on her back to wait for the stars. Night came, and the glittering shards of them studded the black velvet skies.

She felt strangely peaceful now, like someone who had done all they could and at last retired to their much-deserved rest.

As she watched, one of the stars dislodged itself from its dark firmament and began its descent downward, its trajectory burning a path through the night.

Arden followed its luminous trail for as long as she could, and then she closed her eyes.

THE END?

Not if you want to dive into more of Crystal Lake Publishing's Tales from the Darkest Depths!

Check out our amazing website and online store
or download our latest catalog here.
https://geni.us/CLPCatalog

We always have great new projects and content on the website to dive into, as well as a newsletter, behind the scenes options, social media platforms, our own dark fiction shared-world series and our very own webstore. Our webstore even has categories specifically for KU books, non-fiction, anthologies, and of course more novels and novellas.

Dear reader!

Congratulations. You have survived The Island. Or have you? Check to see if you're experiencing any unusual urges or appetites. You can never be too careful!

As a reader, I'm a huge fan of afterwords, so as I writer, I always add one at the end of every publication. If you'd like to learn a bit more about me and my book, read on.

I don't have any memories of a life without books. I learned to read at a very early age, and since then, my life has always been shaped and defined by books—although it took me a very long time to realize that what I really wanted to do was write them. Until that fateful summer of 2021, I was reading and reviewing books like a fiend, averaging 40 to 50 a month. And it was seeing a lot of the same things, in different wrappers.

I get it: publishing is a business like any other. It craves a successful formula. But as a reader, I crave originality most of all. I think that was what pushed me in front of a blank WORD document and inspired me to cover it in stories. Which is to say, I write for very selfish reasons. I simply sit down and write myself stories I want to read.

It's enormously rewarding to have my work get out into the world and find an appreciative audience, but I am my first intended reader and my harshest critic. (My wife is my second reader, and the one I'm proudest and happiest to entertain.)

Writing professionally is hard. Not following convention or market demands makes things harder. But I do think it creates good books, and in the end, that's all that matters.

I'm very grateful that Crystal Lake Publishing recognizes that and supports my work, both with short stories and now a novel.

One of the things I do is set myself challenges. And one of my favorite challenges is to take a well-worn trope and make it into something completely original. (I literally don't think I've ever met a trope I didn't want to subvert!) That was how *Beautiful, Once* came to be. I've read so much zombie fiction over the years - most of it followed the same plot and was forgotten almost immediately. The ones that stuck with me are the ones that did something unique.

Let's face it: it's much easier to write the bite/stab/shoot in the head people vs. zombies than come up with something like *World War Z* or *The Girl with All the Gifts*.

Alternatively, if it isn't entirely original in concept, then it has to wow on other levels. *The Walking Dead* empire has largely understood that by creating a uniquely human-centric zombie apocalypse and knowing who the real monsters are.

For me, at the heart of any good story is a heart. It's that simple. Few horror stories are as inherently human as zombie stories, because confronted with such aggressively outward expressions of their mortality, people can really get to the true meaning of being alive. And so, I wanted to write a uniquely "human" zombie story, from all perspectives.

So, that's half of it. The other half comes from my love of dystopian fiction. Why dystopias? Well, because the poets tell us that "things fall apart, the center cannot hold," and the Second Law of Thermodynamics speaks of entropy, and the news confirms our worst suspicions every single day. Because everything was beautiful, once. Because it's darkly, morbidly fascinating to see how ugly things can become. Because on an intellectual level, as a writer, I like to see how things are made, and the best way to figure that out is by taking them apart.

Dystopias are hubris's folly. So are utopias. The latter cannot be sustained, but the former endures. Things fall apart. Just ask Ronan Bard. Or anyone on his beautiful island.

It also stands to mention that, as a writer, I do another thoroughly unmarketable thing: I genre-hop. It seems unfathomable to me to get locked in a single genre, when I read, think, and create so widely across so many. This novel gave the opportunity to blend at least three: science fiction, thriller, and horror. It's literary too, but that usually goes without saying as all my fiction is, first and foremost, literary. But make no mistake, this is quite possibly the most "horrific" of all my horror, which has often been described as "quiet."

Beautiful, Once, then, is very much my "Hear Me Roar" offering. I hope you enjoyed it!

Every book was just a WORD document on a computer once. It takes a small village to bring it to life. I'd like to thank the villagers—such a nice bunch, not a pitchfork in sight!

My heartfelt gratitude goes out to:

Joe Mynhardt and the entire Crystal Lake team for all their hard work and professional excellence;

All the lovely friends I've made along this writing journey for the steadfast encouragement, banter, and support;

Michael Marshall Smith for his friendship, advice, and most flattering estimation of my writing talents;

Nate Ragolia for the best cheerleading ever;

Davida De La Harpe Golden, my eagle-eyed BETA reader;

Atticus Morton, my wonderful patron of the arts;

And most importantly, my beautiful wife Chelsea, who turns this dystopian world into a utopia every day.

ABOUT THE AUTHOR

Mia Dalia is an internationally published, Crime Writers Association-nominated author of all things fantastic, thrilling, scary, and strange. Her short stories of horror, noir, science fiction, mystery, crime, humor, and more have been featured in a variety of anthologies, magazines, literary journals, online, and adapted for narrative podcasts.

Mia's stories were selected as one of Tales to Terrify's Top Ten Stories of 2023 and shortlisted for the Crime Writers' Association's 2024 Dagger Award. Her work has been acclaimed by *Library Journal,* which "highly recommended it for gothic fiction readers and fans of Shirley Jackson," praised by Kirkus Reviews for its "imaginative directness reminiscent of Stephen King," and lauded by Booklist for its "beautifully detailed characters and a subtle slide into dread."

Mia is the author of the novels *Estate Sale* and *Haven,* the novellas *Alakazam, Tell Me a Story, Discordant, Arrokoth,* and *Do You Know the Muffin Man?* and the collection *Smile So Red and Other Tales of Madness.*

Readers . . .

Thank you for reading *Beautiful, Once*. We hope you enjoyed this novel.

If you have a moment, please review *Beautiful, Once* at the store where you bought it.

Help other readers by telling them why you enjoyed this book. No need to write an in-depth discussion. Even a single sentence will be greatly appreciated. Reviews go a long way to helping a book sell, and is great for an author's career. It'll also help us to continue publishing quality books.

Thank you again for taking the time to journey with Crystal Lake Publishing.

Visit our Linktree page for a list of our social media platforms. https://linktr.ee/CrystalLakePublishing

Follow us on Amazon:

your world, doors within your mind, from talented authors who sacrifice so much for a moment of your time.

There are some amazing small presses out there, and through collaboration and open forums we will continue to support other presses in the goal of helping authors and showing the world what quality small presses are capable of accomplishing. No one wins when a small press goes down, so we will always be there to support hardworking, legitimate presses and their authors. We don't see Crystal Lake as the best press out there, but we will always strive to be the best, strive to be the most interactive and grateful, and even blessed press around. No matter what happens over time, we will also take our mission very seriously while appreciating where we are and enjoying the journey.

What do we offer our authors that they can't do for themselves through self-publishing?

We are big supporters of self-publishing (especially hybrid publishing), if done with care, patience, and planning. However, not every author has the time or inclination to do market research, advertise, and set up book launch strategies. Although a lot of authors are successful in doing it all, strong small presses will always be there for the authors who just want to do what they do best: write.

What we offer is experience, industry knowledge, contacts and trust built up over years. And due to our strong brand and trusting fanbase, every Crystal Lake book comes with weight of respect. In time our fans begin to trust our judgment and will try a new author purely based on our support of said author.

To date we've published around 300 books, and with each launch we strive to fine-tune our approach, learn from our mistakes, and increase our reach. We continue to assure our authors that we're here for them and that we'll carry the weight of the launch and deal with third parties while they focus on their strengths—be it writing, interviews, blogs, signings, etc.

We also offer several mentoring packages to authors that include knowledge and skills they can use in both traditional and self-publishing endeavors. This includes Shadows & Ink Creators on our The House of Shadows & Ink YouTube channel and our Crystal Lake Academy.

We look forward to launching many new careers.

This is what we believe in. What we stand for. This will be our legacy.

Welcome to Crystal Lake Publishing— Where Stories Come Alive!

9 781968 532475